The Detective Is Already Dead

La detective
está muerta.

1

nigozyu

Illustration by **Umibouzu**

D0569967

"I want you to find out who I'm looking for."

Nagisa Natsunagi

"Kimizuka—didn't you have any intention of inheriting Ma'am's job?"

Charlotte Arisaka Anderson

Siesta

Real name	Undisclosed
Age	Unreleased
Nationality	Unrevealed
Birthday	April 2
Likes	Black tea
Dislikes	Waking up early
Hobbies	Napping, teasing her assistant
Calling	Ace detective
Weapon	Musket
Code	Protecting the client's interests

Gifted with both intelligence and beauty,

artless and lovely, absolutely perfect—

Just by appearing,

she makes birds sing and flowers bloom,

and the case is closed before it truly opens.

The Detective Is Already Dead

1

nigozyu

Illustration by Umibouzu

YEN ON

New York

The Detective Is Already Dead, Vol. 1

nigozyu

Translation by Taylor Engel
Cover art by Umibouzu

TANTEI HA MO, SHINDEIRU. Vol.1
©nigozyu 2019
Published in Japan in 2019 by KADOKAWA CORPORATION, Tokyo.
English translation rights arranged with KADOKAWA CORPORATION, Tokyo, through TUTTLE-MORI AGENCY, INC., Tokyo.

English translation © 2021 by Yen Press, LLC

Yen On
150 West 30th Street, 19th Floor
New York, NY 10001

Visit us at yenpress.com
facebook.com/yenpress
twitter.com/yenpress
yenpress.tumblr.com
instagram.com/yenpress

First Yen On Edition: June 2021

Yen On is an imprint of Yen Press, LLC.
The Yen On name and logo are trademarks of Yen Press, LLC.

Library of Congress Cataloging-in-Publication Data
Names: nigozyu, author. | Umibouzu, illustrator. | Engel, Taylor, translator.
Title: The detective is already dead / nigozyu ; illustration by Umibouzu ; translation by Taylor Engel.
Other titles: Tantei wa Mou, Shindeiru. English
Description: First Yen On edition. | New York, NY : Yen On, 2021.
Identifiers: LCCN 2021012132 | ISBN 9781975325756 (v. 1 ; trade paperback)
Subjects: GSAFD: Mystery fiction.
Classification: LCC PL873.5.I46 T3613 2021 | DDC 895.63/6—dc23
LC record available at https://lccn.loc.gov/2021012132

ISBNs: 978-1-9753-2575-6 (paperback)
       978-1-9753-2576-3 (ebook)

10 9 8 7 6 5 4 3 2 1

LSC-C

Printed in the United States of America

The Detective Is Already Dead

1

characters La detective está muerta.

"Perfect timing. You—be my assistant."

Kimihiko Kimizuka
Age 18
Detective's assistant.

Nagisa Natsunagi
Age 18
High school student.

"That's not fair at all! You're the one who press-ganged me, all right?!"

"If you say you're leaving now, I'll double-kill you."

Siesta
(Code name. Real name unknown.)
Age Unknown (Deceased)
Detective.

"I'm the world's *cutest* idol, Yui Saikawa!"

"It's been a while, you damn kid. Finally decided to turn yourself in?"

Charlotte
Arisaka
Anderson
Age 17
Detective's apprentice.

Bat
Age 34
Former enemy.

"...I'd appreciate it if you didn't call me by my nickname."

"Guess why I hijacked the plane."

Yui Saikawa
Age 14
A nationally popular idol singer.

Fuubi Kase
Age 28
Police detective.

Contents

Prologue 1

Chapter 1 5

At the beginning of the mystery,
cop a feel 5

Assistant and client; the detective
is out 7

Say, whose heart is this? 11

This is not a date, of course... 16

Blow your head off 19

No, not that kind
of euphemism 23

Heart, Bat, and pseudohuman 25

Is there a detective on the
plane? 28

Hijacker vs. ace detective 32

Mystery meets sci-fi/fantasy 38

Even now, I remember 45

The detective is already dead 51

A girl's monologue 1 57

One day, two years ago 59

Chapter 2 67

That's right—she's the
self-proclaimed "cutest idol" 67

A simple job: Protect a three-
billion-yen family treasure 70

I won't die 75

The gossip doesn't stop 78

That's "Yui-nya Quality" 81

Sunday showdown 86

Sapphire ★ Phantasm 88

Thus spoke the super-idol 93

What that eye sees 96

More than any idol 100

Because you said "Let's go
to the beach" 107

A girl's monologue 2 113

One day, one year ago 115

Chapter 3 121

Yesterday's enemy is today's
enemy, too 121

Welcome to hell, the land
of dreams 125

That's why I can't be
a detective 128

Cinderella before midnight 131

The worst happens 138

How to use a three-billion-yen
family treasure 142

Light in the midst of hope
(despair) 146

A golden banner flying in
the night sky 154

Buenos días 161

Those unforgettable three years
I spent with you were... 169

The girls' dialogue 181

Epilogue 185

Afterword 193

Prologue

"Is there a detective on the plane?"

...I didn't hear that right, I thought.

You don't often get that question on a passenger plane cruising at roughly ten thousand meters, after all. I must have misheard or misinterpreted somehow. Maybe it was the altitude?

"Nah, probably not."

I nixed my own idea and calmed down a little, then looked around and saw that a flustered cabin attendant was marching this way.

"Is there a detective on the plane?"

Apparently, I wasn't imagining things.

Geez, not again.

For as long as I can remember, I've had an incredible knack for running into trouble. I guess you could say I was born for it.

When I walk down major streets, I get stuck in the middle of flash mobs. When I take back alleys, I stumble onto transactions involving a suspicious white powder. I've run into the same cops at so many murder scenes that we know each other by sight, and I'm always a suspect. Today, as it happens, I was flying overseas with a really big attaché case, and I didn't have a clue what was in it.

And I was only in my second year of middle school. Maybe one day I'd be a spy or in the military.

As if. I wanna work a desk job for the government and actually go home at closing time. Don't expect any heroism from me, all right?

And so:

"Of course there isn't."

What was going on here anyway? Ordinarily, you'd expect them to ask for a doctor or nurse.

We've all heard the line before, on TV or in comics: *Is there a doctor in the house?* Right now, though, what they were asking for way up here in the sky was—a detective? That made no sense.

Exactly what kind of situation would require a detective on an airplane in flight? Nope, no way. I refused to get dragged into even more trouble I didn't need.

Ignoring the incoming cabin attendant, I shut my eyes tight.

Right after that, it happened.

"Yes, I'm a detective."

The voice carried so well that my eyes opened on their own, just in time to see a girl about my age raise her hand from the seat on my right.

Her bobbed hair was pale silver, and her enchanting blue eyes pulled you in. Her dress was a flattering color, apparently modeled on some country's military uniform, and the glimpses of skin I caught beneath it were as clear as snow.

She was so beautiful she could have been an angel incarnate. If you looked up *beauty* in the dictionary, her name was bound to be there. If you ran a search of her name online, you can bet the related images would have been photos of flowers and birds and the moon.

Which was why all my interest just then was focused on learning what her name actually was.

Detective? Whatever, I don't care. Who is this girl? That's I want to know.

"What's your name?"

So the next thing I knew, I'd asked her aloud.

…But even now, four years later, I still don't know what her name was. At least, not her real one. All she told me was her alias: "Siesta."

She was a real detective who fought "the enemies of the world."

After that, I became her assistant, and we set off on a journey together.

"Ready?" she'd say. "While they're filling you full of lead, I'll go take down the enemy leader."

"Hey, ace detective," I'd say, "you wanna make a plan that gets both of us out alive?"

"Don't worry—I'll erase your computer's search history."

"...Hold it. You looked at my history? You looked at my search history?!"

Eventually, we were close enough that we could banter easily. We spent three full years on a kaleidoscopic adventure—

—and then death tore us apart.

It's been a year since then, so four years total.

I'm the one who got to live. My name is Kimihiko Kimizuka, and at eighteen, I'm currently in my last year of high school. And my life is now completely, utterly normal. Tepid and routine.

Am I okay with that, you ask?

Sure. It's not like I'm causing trouble for anybody.

I mean, it's true, isn't it?

The detective is already dead.

Chapter 1

◆ At the beginning of the mystery, cop a feel

"You're the ace detective?"

Class was done for the day, and the sun was going down. In a classroom, someone had hauled me up by my shirtfront and right out of my nap to interrogate me.

My bleary eyes couldn't really make out her face. I checked back through my memories, but I didn't recognize her voice.

Apparently, I was being threatened by some girl I didn't know. I had no clue why.

I'd spent the whole school day, from the morning bell until class was over, facedown on my desk. This girl struck me as the type who'd run for student government; maybe she couldn't stand seeing her classmate sleep his life away and had done me the favor of waking me up but got a little rough...or something?

No, if we were in the same class, I would at least remember her voice.

This girl really was a total stranger to me.

Then what was this? Why was I being hauled up by my collar? And the progressive tense there is literal—she was still holding me.

My sleep-addled brain wasn't up to deducing much of anything. Of course it wasn't; I'm no detective.

Wait, detective?

Didn't this girl say "detective" a minute ago?

"Don't just stand there—answer me. Are you Kimihiko Kimizuka, the ace detective people are talking about?"

It was the first time in a year that I'd heard that awful word. *Detective.*

"You've got the wrong guy. Now, if you'll excuse me…"

"Wait."

"Gweh," I wheezed. Humans normally aren't supposed to make sounds like that.

Impossible as it was to believe, she'd shoved her fingers into my mouth.

"If you're going to ignore my question, don't expect mercy. I'll touch the dangly thing at the back of your throat."

"This's…really unfair…"

Finally, I got a clear look at her face.

Strong-willed and sharp eyes. Long eyelashes. A prominent nose and tense lips.

A little of her long black hair was pulled into a stylish ponytail high on the side of her head, like any contemporary high school girl.

…But I didn't remember anyone like her going to my school. *I can't believe I didn't even notice such a dangerous character. I guess I'm not as sharp as I used to be.*

"So you are Kimihiko Kimizuka, right?"

Hearing my full name over and over felt weird. Reluctantly, I nodded.

"Answer me properly. Use your words."

"…Khah!"

Her fingertips touched my uvula, and bile welled up from the pit of my stomach.

"Ugh, you're the worst. Getting this much spit all over the fingers of a girl you've just met—what is wrong with you?"

I wanted to ask her who put the fingers in my mouth in the first place, but they were still touching the back of my mouth, and her other hand was gripping my uniform shirt. It was practically a new type of torture.

"Guh…ungh…"

"Huh? Come on, you're crying? A big boy of eighteen, and getting a girl's fingers all sticky with your drool isn't enough for you? You want to cry and throw a tantrum? You had other ways you wanted to play?"

I could hear my dignity as a human being crashing down around me. I couldn't blink back the tears or swallow the drool. What the hell? What did I do to deserve this?

"Oh, I see. Yes, of course: *You wanted me to hold you close, didn't you?*"

She pressed my face to her chest.

The marshmallowy softness and the sweet scent of her perfume threatened to dissolve my brain.

And the sound of her heart— That's weird. For some reason, it seemed terribly familiar. Could I possibly be sensing something maternal in a girl my own age?

...Nope. No way. Not touching that.

Caught between pleasure and agony, I yelled and wrenched myself free.

"That's too bad. I wouldn't have minded playing with you for a bit longer."

".........*Hff...hff,* don't use your body to play games with people. Don't push some stranger's face into your boobs," I snapped

For the first time, she smiled faintly. "I'm Nagisa Natsunagi," she said. The name was seasonally appropriate—meaning "calm summer shore"—and she held out her right hand for me to shake.

"...Go wash that first, all right?"

◆ Assistant and client; the detective is out

"I'd like to place a request."

A few minutes later, Natsunagi had returned from the bathroom and taken the seat in front of me so that we were facing each other.

"Don't you have something to say to me first?"

"Yes, I'd like to request an apology for getting my fingers dirty."

"*I'm* supposed to apologize?!"

Again, she was being totally unfair. It was so unfair that you could pull together all the unfairness in the world and still not have enough to cover it.

"Well, when you do something people don't like, offering an apology is the natural course of action, isn't it?"

"It sure as hell is, so I could say the same to you!"

"Oh, come on. Anyone would think I'd done something to you that you didn't like."

Yeah, actually—that's exactly what I've been saying!

What is her deal? Is this girl trying to improv a comedy sketch with me a few minutes after we've just met?

"You're saying you wouldn't mind if somebody pulled a stunt like that on you?" I asked.

"Huh? ...Th-that's a good question." Natsunagi's gaze abruptly began to wander. "You're right; I guess I wouldn't want someone doing that to me. That's normal. Yeah..."

"Huh? Why are you blushing a little? What was that last part supposed to mean?"

Hey, her sadist character just evaporated. As a matter of fact, I was starting to wonder whether she was compensating.

...Maybe I should check.

"Would you rather be loved, or...?"

"Love."

"Would you rather tie up someone else, or...?"

"Be tied up."

"Money's tight this month, so..."

"I'll pay. How much do you need?"

"Wow, you're *really* a masochist."

"Wha—?!" Natsunagi's lips trembled as if I'd just confronted her with a shocking revelation.

Seriously, what happened to the girl I was talking to a few seconds ago?

"I-I'm not! I don't have...*preferences* like that! ...And hey, would you not derail the conversation? I'm here because I have a request for you!"

Was it anger, embarrassment, or the sunset light creating the flush on her cheeks? Natsunagi smacked the desk and stood up. *So her default is being aggressive, then.*

For a little while after that, her shoulders were heaving as she caught her breath.

"I'm looking for someone," she said. Her eyes were incredibly serious.

I see, a missing person. That's why she wanted an ace detective, hmm?

"You are Kimihiko Kimizuka...aren't you?"

...Geez. She's not going to let me go until she gets an answer.

"Yes. I've been a Kimizuka since before I was born, and I've been a Kimihiko since the day of."

"And you're an ace detective?"

"Unfortunately, you've got the wrong guy. I don't have a granddad who was a detective, and I've never been force-fed a weird drug and ended up looking like a little kid."

"The wrong guy?" Natsunagi's eyebrows jumped. "But I saw it in the paper."

"The paper?"

When I heard that, I thought back...but I didn't know *what Natsunagi was referring to.*

"The evening edition three days ago, about an admirable high school boy who caught a bag snatcher."

"Oh, that, huh?"

"Yes—but if that was all, I wouldn't be doing this." Then Natsunagi opened her school bag and upended it, dumping its contents all over the floor. "These are all articles about you."

It was a massive number of newspaper clippings.

"...You checked into me?"

Each of the articles had my name and headshot... Well, that was part of why I asked; I hadn't known *which incident* Natsunagi had seen in the paper.

"Um, 'Super high school boy shuts down billing fraud before it happens!' 'Finding pets is his specialty: Boy K. locates another lost kitten.' 'Life-saving expert saves two lives on his way to school!' —If you insist you're not an ace detective, what in the world are you?"

This is what my routine looks like these days. I still get dragged into things constantly, and by now, I'm completely used to it.

I didn't think that would necessarily make me an "ace detective," but... Well, I knew what she was trying to say.

"You're exaggerating. C'mon, don't overestimate me."

The fact that I run into incidents, and that I luck into resolving them, is all due to the way trouble always finds me. It's not like I have any special skills.

Way back when, those experiences did make me overconfident. However, a year ago, I was forced to see that they were absolutely worthless.

So I don't want anybody thinking I can do more than I can. Sorry, but I'm no detective. Right now, I'm pretty sure this tepid life suits me best.

"How modest," Natsunagi said.

"Gee, thanks."

"That wasn't a compliment."

"What, it wasn't?!"

"You can't even see your own abilities right; why would I compliment you?"

Aha. Apparently, that had been her brand of sarcasm.

"Well, if even I can't see my own abilities right, what makes you think someone else can do better?"

"You're saying no one can know you better than you? Awfully full of yourself." Natsunagi crossed her arms, hugging her own chest, and gave a little snort. "Subjective opinions are the least reliable things in the world. What's important is always objective fact. Am I wrong?" Natsunagi asked, yanking on my shirt again and pulling me toward her.

Her moist lips were right there. Her breath was sweet and warm. Her ruby-red eyes were boring a hole right between mine.

She continued. "The things you did are solid fact. That means how we praise those achievements, and how they compare with others, is entirely up to 'someone else.' Don't you think?"

Her straightforward, haughty gaze reminded me very strongly of someone else. Someone who didn't exist anymore.

"...So you said you were looking for somebody?" Yeah, I'd had all I could take of being that close. I pushed Natsunagi's shoulders away, and we stood facing each other.

"Yes...?"

I know; she got me good. But for the sake of my pride, let me stress that Natsunagi hadn't argued me down or persuaded me in any particular way.

It was just that now that I'd seen *that shadow of someone else* in her, it was all I could do.

Geez. I'm well trained, huh?

"You'll accept the role of detective?" Suddenly, the emotion on Natsunagi's face turned to shock. There was something unexpectedly childlike about the way her expression changed from moment to moment.

"No, I can't be a detective. But—"

"But?"

"If you'll settle for an assistant, I'll take the job."

Natsunagi gave a wry, chagrined smile. "What's that supposed to mean?"

Sorry, but that's been my position for four years. "And? Who are you looking for?" *Just finding someone shouldn't take all that long,* I thought and stretched.

With a perfectly straight face, Natsunagi replied, "Good question. I don't know. *I want you to find out who I'm looking for.*"

Well, I suppose that tracked. For a girl who'd declared that subjective opinions were the least reliable things in the world, it was a very appropriate problem.

◆ Say, whose heart is this?

"So then, what? You're saying you've had this constant feeling that you're forgetting someone lately, but you can't remember who?"

On the way home, after that conversation, Natsunagi and I had stopped in at a café, and we were discussing her request again over coffee.

"Right. There's somebody I absolutely have to find and talk to, but I have no idea who they are. I couldn't even begin to guess their age or gender, or where they live... Ooh, this is good."

Smiling faintly, Natsunagi raised her mug to her lips. Even just caffeinating herself, she was as pretty as a picture. Lucky her.

As for me, I have no idea how many times my old partner told me she'd forget my boring face if she didn't see it for a couple of days.

"...What? Why are you staring at me like that?" Natsunagi finally seemed to have registered my gaze; she pushed her chair back a bit. Stealing glances at me, she fidgeted with the hem of her short skirt.

"You want to be watched?"

"...—!"

Something whacked me over the head, like a paper fan from a slapstick show.

"…You're being unfair."

"You've been making a lot of weird assumptions for a while now, Kimizuka… And is 'unfair' a speech tic of yours or something?"

"When someone's being unfair, I have to say so. That's all."

It's why I was saying it for the first time *in a year*. I didn't actually want to, you know.

"All right, getting back on topic." I took a swallow of my coffee, too. "This mystery person you're looking for—let's call them 'X.' You don't have even the tiniest clue about X?"

"Nope. I don't even know why I'm so obsessed. It's just…at random moments, I start wanting to see them. Even though I don't know who they are." Natsunagi gazed out the window.

"Roughly when did this start? Has it been this way for as long as you can remember, or since you started high school, or…?"

"One year ago." She seemed very sure about that.

Natsunagi said she didn't know X's gender or nationality or age, but apparently she was certain about when she'd started thinking about them.

"What happened a year ago?"

"I almost died, but I didn't. Well, to be more specific, someone gave me my life."

If she'd gone out of her way to rephrase, the point was significant.

For some reason, Natsunagi's life had been in peril, but this wasn't the language you'd use to describe a narrow escape. In that case—

"The heartbeat I let you hear in the classroom—*that wasn't mine.*"

"—An organ transplant, huh?"

Natsunagi gave a small nod. "I've had a heart ailment ever since I was little. While I waited for the day they could do the transplant, I was in and out of the hospital all the time… I couldn't even go to school."

"I see. No wonder I didn't know you."

"Right. After all, you couldn't possibly have missed such an adorable girl otherwise."

"Sorry, I've had this big chunk of earwax plugging my ear since yesterday, so I can't hear... Ow, ow, ow, ow! Don't grab my little finger! Stop squeezing—you'll break it!"

"Well, you're the one who broke the conversation."

"That argument makes zero sense!"

You get to be a sadist or a masochist, not both. Don't get greedy.

I sighed, but Natsunagi ignored me and went on.

"Then, one year ago, they found a compatible donor, and I was finally able to receive a heart transplant. That's when I started to get flickers of X's presence in the back of my mind."

"You mean you've already been looking for a year?"

"No. I had to be on bed rest for a while after the transplant; even if I'd wanted to do something about it, I couldn't. But I finally started going to school recently, and I'd read articles about you, Kimizuka."

I see. I was finally getting a picture of the time line and the rough shape of events. We might be able to clear up this issue a lot sooner than I thought.

"Memory transference," I said.

Natsunagi tilted her head slightly. Apparently, it was a foreign concept to her.

In that case, putting it like this might make it easier to understand.

"This X you're looking for—they're someone *the former owner of your heart* wants to see."

"...That's the craziest thing I've ever..."

"If you really think so, then why was your heart transplant the first thing you told me about?"

Natsunagi fell silent.

"You said you'd started to sense X's shadow a year ago. When I asked what had happened back then, you said an organ transplant had saved your life. So you yourself just admitted that there's a correlation between X and your heart transplant. Am I wrong?"

"...You're kind of a jerk, Kimizuka."

Natsunagi glared at me from under half-lowered eyelids. Guess I was right.

"The phenomenon of memory transference hasn't been scientifically proved, but there have been multiple cases of it. In 1988, a Jewish woman named Claire Sylvia received an organ transplant in America, and a few days later, her eating habits changed drastically. She developed a taste for peppers, which she'd never liked, and for fast food, even though she was a ballet dancer who always used to avoid it. Later, when she talked to her donor's family, she learned that those were things he'd liked."

"That could have been coincidence, couldn't it?"

"That's not all. In her dreams, Claire saw her donor's first name. She asked his family, and that was indeed his name. And that's just one of many... Want more?"

"...You're kind of a jerk, Kimizuka."

It didn't matter what she thought of me; if she was convinced, that was fine.

"So what? Does that mean *this heart is the one who wants to meet X*, not me?"

"Probably. I'm guessing X is the donor's family member, lover, or friend... Something along those lines."

"I see..." Natsunagi slipped a hand over the left side of her chest, biting her lip softly.

"Well, there you go: Congratulations. Problem solved."

Well, I helped her out this far. She can pay me in coffee.

On that thought, I got up, leaving the bill, but...

"Huh? Where do you think you're going?" Natsunagi was glaring daggers at me. "If you say you're leaving now, I'll double-kill you."

"That's very...original. Geez, okay." Cowed by her hostility, I reluctantly returned to my chair. "I thought the conversation was over."

"What gave you that idea? Weren't you looking at a girl who'd put her hand on her chest, biting her lip forlornly?"

"I thought you were just indulging in a sentimental epilogue."

"You have no human feelings, do you?"

Human feelings? Nah, I threw those away in a back alley somewhere a year ago.

"Think what you want. Natsunagi, like I said, the owner of that heart is the one who wants to meet X, not you. It's just a memory from when they were alive. This has nothing to do with you."

"You're wrong!" Natsunagi smacked the table and stood up. "That's wrong. This isn't just a memory—it's a regret. Even if their body is dead, they let me inherit their heart. That's how badly they want to meet X. This heart gave me life, and I want to pay it back. It's the least I can do. I want to help this heart find who it's looking for."

The way she spoke had changed from what it had been earlier. It was proof that she was saying what she really felt, compelled by her emotions.

"So all this is really for yourself."

"Sure, I'm doing it for myself. This heart is mine. That means I'm the one who wants to see X."

"That's not what you said before."

"...Just shut up and help me."

A moist towelette came flying across the table, thwacked me in the face, and clung there. It was indeed moist and really gross.

"...I assume you're going to compensate me?"

When I peeled the wet cloth off my face, my eyes met Natsunagi's grumpy ones.

"I paid you in advance by letting you touch my chest, remember?"

"Classic extortion."

"If that's not enough for you, I'll expose your weird habits to the entire student body."

"And like I said, I could sure as hell say the same to you!"

"Ngh... Listen, do you think I really am *one of those people*...?"

"If you want someone to give you advice, that is the literal worst way to go about it."

Nonsense aside...

"Well, I did say I'd do it."

I'd already agreed, and I couldn't really go back on my word.

"No matter what, the client's interests must be protected."

That's something *she* used to tell me, over and over.

"All right then, tomorrow. We'll meet in front of the station at two in the afternoon."

"Huh? Tomorrow?"

"Yeah. It's already late today."

Left with no choice, I took the check and got up, getting ready to leave.

"You want to see X, right?"

◆ This is not a date, of course...

"Sorry to keep you waiting."

It was the weekend, and I'd been standing in the shadow of a pillar on the station-front plaza, checking my watch, when something thumped me lightly on the shoulder.

When I turned around, there was Natsunagi, dressed in street clothes and swinging a small handbag around.

Her off-the-shoulder blouse generously exposed her white collarbones, and her denim shorts highlighted her long, slim legs. It was as if she'd dressed for the "summer" that was part of her name.

"Can you stop eyeing up a female classmate who isn't even your girlfriend?"

"Not sure I want to hear that from someone who shoved her boobs against a classmate who wasn't even her boyfriend."

"You liked it, though."

"......"

Damn. She got me there.

"Never mind that. Natsunagi, you're ten minutes late. Be punctual." Since I couldn't deny her accusation, I changed the subject.

"Girls need their time to get ready, no matter what they're doing." Natsunagi pouted, and there was vivid lipstick on those lips.

I see; that's true. She looked about 30 percent more grown-up than she did the day before.

"That so? Sorry."

"You're awfully cooperative now."

"Well, I appreciate having a pretty girl next to me, too."

"...Hmph. I don't mind hearing that," Natsunagi murmured, looking up through her lashes at me from about ten centimeters below.

"...What?"

"Nothing..."

"Come on, what?!"

"Nothiiing."

No, seriously, what the heck?

I looked down at Natsunagi, whose position made her boobs impossible to miss.

"......Staring much?" Natsunagi glared at me coldly, hugging herself. The tables had turned.

"No, not your boobs. I was just, you know, observing your collarbones."

"Ew! At least check out my boobs like a normal person!"

"You've got a fine pair for somebody your age."

"What does age have to do with collarbones?! Why are you talking like some collarbone critic?! ...What even is a collarbone critic anyway?!"

"...Hmm. Have we had a conversation like this before?" I asked.

"I sure hope not; once is way more than enough for me." Harried, Natsunagi pressed a hand against her forehead. "...Hey, when did I get cast as the character who makes all the comebacks?"

"It's good to switch up the roles every once in a while." Well, to be honest, it's not like I really wanted that position, either. "Okay, we should head out." I smacked Natsunagi on the shoulder and set off, taking the lead.

"Where are you going? Listen, they'll arrest you unless you put some clothes on."

"Hey, if you want to steal the funny role back, you need more buildup."

...Still, this is weird.

Oddly, when Natsunagi joked around, it struck a chord in me.

After we'd walked for about ten minutes, our destination came into view.

"Um, Kimizuka? I'm pretty sure I've got the wrong idea, but is that where we're going?"

"We're looking for someone. So this isn't all that weird."

Even so, Natsunagi frowned, seeming unconvinced. "Are you planning to have them look for X?"

"No, we're laying the groundwork. If you want to shoot the general, first shoot his horse."

"The general is X... So the horse is...the heart?"

"Right. First, we're going to check into the donor who saved your life."

This "X" that Natsunagi was looking for had to have been close to the heart's former owner.

In that case, pinpointing who the donor was would have to come first.

"Then shouldn't we be going to a hospital?"

"I'd love to, but unfortunately, I don't have any medical connections."

"...That means you do know somebody here."

"Well, don't get so tense. C'mon, we're going in."

And so we stepped into the towering skyscraper that housed *the Metropolitan Police Department.*

◆ Blow your head off

"Hey. It's been a while, you damn kid. Finally decided to turn yourself in?"

A woman finally entered the room where we were waiting and dropped heavily onto the sofa across from Natsunagi and me, kicking out her long legs in a lazy way.

"Ms. Fuubi, I'm not sure women should sit with their legs spread like that."

"Shove it. Gender's got nothin' to do with getting by here." As she spoke, she lit a fat cigar.

Striking was one way to describe her face—*flashy* was another—and she wore her uniform in an incredibly casual way. Her blazing-red hair was pulled back in a messy ponytail.

Nobody who was seeing her for the first time would have believed it, but Fuubi Kase was a police inspector.

Considering the fact that she'd been a beat cop when I first met her five or six years back, for somebody who was (probably) in her late twenties, she seemed to be making good progress in her career.

"So what did you pull this time? Theft? Murder?"

"I haven't done anything. As a matter of fact, I recently got a public commendation for catching another burglar."

"You're the first one on the scene of a solid seventy percent of all the crimes in this district. You really can't blame us for suspecting you stage them."

"It just happens. It's how I'm wired."

My bad luck with Ms. Fuubi began right when she became a police officer and started showing up at crime scenes.

I must have left an impression in her mind as that suspicious kid who was almost always at a murder scene. I'd really love to clear up that misunderstanding, but she still seems to think I'm sketchy.

"It is, huh? And you wired yourself up to a real detective?"

"...No idea. If I had to say, it felt more like she drew me to her, twisted me tight around her little finger, and then went off somewhere far away by herself."

That's right: Extremely far away. Somewhere you couldn't find on any map; a distant, unreachable—

"Hah! Well, that's true." Smiling slightly, Ms. Fuubi gave a husky laugh. "And what about you? You workin' solo now?"

"...No, there's nothing I can do on my own. Besides, it looks like I'm not even on *their* radar; things have been so peaceful it's scary."

"Well, damn. You're pretty heartless. The dead tell no tales, huh?"

I had no intention of saying that much. After all, she'd probably haunt me for it.

"Ow!"

Just then, a sharp pain ran through my foot. When I looked down, Natsunagi's sneaker was stomping on it.

"What was that for?"

"Huh? Oh, um, just for...reasons? And hey, don't shut me out like this."

Don't stomp a guy for "...reasons?" Seriously.

"Uh, so, Ms. Fuubi. Getting down to business, I wanted to speak with you about this girl, my friend—"

"So your girlfriend?"

"No, that's why I said them separately."

Ms. Fuubi's eyes went to Natsunagi, seated beside me.

"It's a pleasure to meet you. My name is Nagisa Natsunagi. I'm here on Mr. Kimizuka's introduction."

"Mr. Kimizuka"... That had a very different ring to it.

And hey, Natsunagi can behave politely in public, huh?

"So you just wanna 'speak with' me and make an 'introduction,' huh? Fine. Let's hear it. Briefly," Ms. Fuubi said and lit her second cigar.

A few minutes later...

"I see."

When we'd finished our story, Ms. Fuubi exhaled one last, long puff of smoke, then stubbed out the butt in the ashtray.

"I get what's going on... But why'd you come *here*?" Narrowing her already sharp eyes even further, she glared at us. "You want us to look for the person who donated her heart? You know we're not doctors, right?"

"Finding people is technically a job for the police."

"Not finding organ donors."

Obviously irritated, Ms. Fuubi crossed her legs.

"There, what did I tell you? This was the wrong place," Natsunagi whispered, jabbing me with her elbow. *Well, just hang on a minute.*

"Police organizations aren't completely disconnected from these incidents. In fact, if the police aren't present, they can't even declare a potential donor brain-dead."

By law, all cases in which brain death is declared have to be reported to the First Investigation Division of the National Police Agency's Criminal Affairs Bureau. Autopsies are also performed under the supervision and direction of the chief of the police station in each jurisdiction. That means, when I chose to come here, I wasn't that far off base. And besides—

"I didn't come to the police. I came to *you*."

Not just anyone would do. This was the kind of thing I could ask because it was Ms. Fuubi.

"And what does that get you?"

"Ms. Fuubi, you aren't like ordinary police officers."

"I'm not? How so?"

"Your resolution."

Or maybe it would be better to say her goals.

This woman isn't like the officers who want money and power. That's why—and I mean this in the kindest way possible—she's not really bound by common sense.

"There's no way I can release a donor's personal information to an average Joe."

"I know."

"Besides, I'm with a different jurisdiction, and my position doesn't come with the authority to disclose information."

"I know that, too."

"Then why did you come to me?"

"Because I figured you'd manage anyway. Since it's you."

"...What's wrong with you?"

Looking a little embarrassed, Ms. Fuubi raked her fingers roughly through her red hair. "Look. You already know I want to get to *the top* here. That means I don't want to run any risks that could trip me up."

"Ha-ha, pretty late to pretend you have common sense, don't you think?"

"I'm gonna blow your head off."

She pointed her gun at my forehead.

"...Um, I pretty sure this would count as a risk."

I mean, take a look. Even Natsunagi is all tense.

"Well, that's how it is. Sorry, sweetheart, but go home, wouldja?" Holstering her gun, Ms. Fuubi stretched.

"No... Please. No matter what it takes, I..."

"You can ask as nicely as you want, but I can't do what I can't do." With that, she stood up, rolling her shoulders. "Besides, I'm busy. I'm scheduled to stop at *the big house* after this."

Big house? ...Oh. I get it now.

Natsunagi seemed confused, but the explanations would have to wait. "You're going to meet somebody?"

Ms. Fuubi stopped, one hand on the door. "Somebody you know real well. So, y'know, *if you're planning to follow me*, it's a free country."

Bingo, huh? Geez, she's the opposite of straightforward.

"Just for the record, let me ask. Does this person have good ears?"

At that, Ms. Fuubi turned back.

"Yeah. *He never forgets the sound of a heart once he's heard it.*"

◆ No, not that kind of euphemism

After the fifteen-minute drive from the Metropolitan Police Department to *the big house*, we followed Ms. Fuubi through *heavy security*, then headed down, deep underground.

We went down stairs, then down more stairs. As we did, the number of lights decreased, and our footsteps echoed more.

"You've only got until I finish my job upstairs. That's about twenty minutes. Can you stick to that?" Ms. Fuubi tossed her question back at us over her shoulder.

"Of course."

Even though she'd shoved us away by pretending not to care what we did, she was showing us the way, which pushed her past "not straightforward" to "way too nice." I mean, she'd actually given us a ride over here in a police car.

"You aren't going to see him, Ms. Fuubi?"

"Ha. No matter what I say, he won't talk. It's a waste of time."

"If he's giving *you* trouble, he must really be something else."

"As if you've got nothing to do with him. You're the one who brought him in."

"I know nothing about that. Tell it to the deceased detective."

"Don't use your partner as a pardon," Ms. Fuubi said, giving my head a little shove. "There you go. We're here."

The air down here on this floor was even more stagnant than the rest of the dark interior. The smell of mold almost made me wrinkle my nose.

"Twenty minutes, you hear? You're not getting any more. You either, sweetheart; understand?"

With that final warning, Ms. Fuubi lightly raised a hand, then started back up the stairs we'd just come down.

The ones she left behind were me and—

"...Um, Kimizuka? Probably should've asked earlier, but weren't we headed to someone's house?"

—Natsunagi, who was looking around a little restlessly.

"Yeah. This *is* the house, Natsunagi."

"Where, exactly?!"

Where? If I had to say, well…

"I mean, it is a prison."

"I noticed that; I'm asking *why!*" Natsunagi pulled on my ear mercilessly. Apparently, she only played innocent in public. "I was visualizing a log cabin–style place, and now we're here in all this concrete with iron bars all over the place."

"Mm-hmm. Because it's a prison."

"What happened to the house, huh?"

"It's a euphemism."

"A-a euphemism?"

"…Now listen…"

Why does she seem a little excited? She's exactly what I thought she was.

"It's a slang term for 'prison.' Sometimes they call it 'the big house' instead. It's common knowledge."

"Common knowledge to who?"

"Common knowledge if you've been flying overseas with attaché cases full of unknown contents since you were in middle school."

"Boy, sure hope I never get to know anybody like that."

You're standing next to one right now.

"So? Why are we here?"

Natsunagi seemed to be more used to the place now. She was looking around, trying to peer in through the iron bars.

"Not over there. She said the one we're here for is all the way at the end." I took the lead, walking in front of Natsunagi.

"Who's here?"

"Some old guy."

"Be serious."

"Some old guy who gave up on being human."

"Well, seeing how he's down here, he might as well have given up his humanity, but…"

"No, that's not what I meant." This was an extremely serious fact, and an irreversible one. "The man we're about to meet is literally *not human.*"

Say this daily routine of mine—of ours—and all the little bits and pieces that aren't routine happened to be a story. If there were people who were hoping that story would be a genuine mystery, I'd like to take the opportunity to apologize. I don't think this story will be what they're here for.

"Kimizuka, that man..." Natsunagi caught the edge of my sleeve hesitantly.

In the very back of the basement, there was a small steel room that was completely enclosed. When we looked in through the only window—a small glass plate in the door—we saw a seated man with chains wrapped around his arms.

After a pause, the shutter door slid open with a dull creak.

"Hey, it's been a long time—Bat."

At the sound of my voice, the man twitched. There was stubble on his chin, and his blond hair was messy. At last, his face slowly, sluggishly turned toward us.

"Now, there's a sound that brings back memories—ace detective."

◆ Heart, Bat, and pseudohuman

I knew this particular jailbird.

His name—his *alias*—was Bat. I never wanted to see this guy again if I could help it.

But as Ms. Fuubi had hinted, he might be able to solve Natsunagi's problem. Reminding myself that this was work, I faced Bat.

"Unfortunately, I'm not an ace detective."

Sorry, but the only ones here are the assistant and a client.

"Hmm? ...Oh, you're— Yeah, I see. Watson, huh?" His unfocused eyes glared at me, and then the corners of his lips quirked up slightly.

"Your Japanese is as good as ever."

"Ha-ha! It's an essential skill for a guy like me. Besides, I've been living here for years now; I've forgotten my mother tongue."

I'm pretty sure he was from northern Europe. However, those rare emerald eyes of his were dull and cloudy now.

"Do your eyes still work?"

"Nah, they're useless at this point. It doesn't really matter to me whether I've got eyes or not, though."

"I hear it matters to most people."

"We've got the same eyes now, Watson. Like a dead fish."

"That's the worst news I've heard this century. Also, I'd appreciate it if you didn't call me that."

"Ha-ha! What, you all done playing assistant?"

...Well, that was the plan anyway. "I'm here because I wanted to talk to you, Bat."

"Huh. I bet. Unless there were special circumstances, there's no way you two would come all the way down here to see me."

You two, huh? True, when I first met this guy, I wasn't alone.

That was a long time ago, though.

"Sure, go ahead and talk. Life in here is boring as hell. It'll make for a good way to kill time." With a hint of life in his voice, Bat urged me to go on.

"I see. In that case, I'll introduce you right away. The girl next to me is Nagisa Natsunagi; she's a classmate of mine."

"Nagisa...Natsunagi?" At that, Bat moved his head slightly, turning those cloudy eyes on the girl next to me.

"...It's a pleasure to meet you. My name is Natsunagi."

She'd briefly flinched, but she promptly resumed her usual resolute expression, facing the prisoner in front of her squarely.

"I came today because I wanted to ask you about my heart."

A few minutes later...

"I see; so that's what it was. No wonder."

When Natsunagi had finished telling him about her problem, Bat cracked his neck audibly.

"Long story short, you came to ask me if I had any idea who owned that heart."

"Yes, that's right... But..." Natsunagi leaned over to whisper in my ear. "Can he actually tell something like that?"

Oh, right. Come to think of it, I hadn't filled Natsunagi in on that part yet.

"Uh, so, he's..."

"Hey, that was pretty rude, sweetheart."

"Ack! He heard us." Natsunagi looked off into the distance, embarrassed.

Well, of course he did. After all—

"Ha-ha! At this distance, I don't even have to try. If I feel like it, I can hear people talking *a hundred kilometers away*."

That's where "Bat" got his code name.

This guy wasn't human. He was part of the group my old partner fought against right up until the moment she died: a pseudohuman.

"Well, *I lost my sight* in exchange. Besides, my phenomenal ears aren't any use in here. As long as the door to this cell is shut, this place is sound-proof. Wonder if this is what the undead feel like? Ha-ha!" Bat's joke at his own expense wasn't very funny. "Now that I can use my ears, though, picking up the sound of your heart is a cakewalk for me."

"That's crazy..."

"Some things are, y'know. Big world out there." Bat smiled at Natsunagi.

It sounded like a good argument, but it wasn't. He was still as good as ever at messing with your head when you talked to him. That had to be why Ms. Fuubi had been so adamant about putting a time limit on our visit.

"...Let's say I believe you. What are you planning to do, after you listen to my heart?"

Although she was still wary, Natsunagi prompted Bat to go on.

"I've got a database of the hearts of all the people I've met over the past few decades. I'll check it against that and see if I find any hits."

"That's the craziest thing I've ever—! And what even are the chances that you just conveniently ran into the owner of this heart before...?"

"No, Natsunagi. It may be safe to get our hopes up a little."

"Kimizuka? What do you mean?"

After all, this guy didn't have an ordinary career. He was a pseudo-human who flew all over the world, following *orders*.

It was possible he met the owner of Natsunagi's heart while they were alive. And, using his augmented ears with their extraordinarily sharp hearing, he could even tell different heartbeats apart. That's an ability he really has.

"I wasn't trying to hide it from you, Natsunagi, but I know this man well. I first met him *four years ago*—above the clouds, at ten thousand meters."

That's right. It was that day—the day I met the ace detective.

This guy was a fellow passenger on that plane.

"Ha-ha, has it been four years already? That takes me back... Hey, why don't we reminisce for a bit?" Bat's dull eyes gleamed slightly.

"Sorry, but we don't have that kind of time. Ms. Fuubi gave us a set visitation window."

"Oh, the broad with an ass as big as her attitude? Eh, it'll be fine. How about I slip you a little intel about *us* afterward? You'll be able to put her in a good mood that way."

"What are you trying to pull, Bat?"

I know they say not to look a gift horse in the mouth, but he was being way too cooperative. Even if banter was part of our relationship, Bat and I were definitely not on the same team.

"I'm not trying to pull anything. It's just been a long time since I had guests, so my mood's a bit better than normal."

And I'm supposed to believe that?

...Still, if we put him in a bad mood at this point, we could end up wasting our hard-won hint.

"Sorry, Natsunagi. This is going to take a little while."

Geez. If that's how it is, no way to go but forward.

I thought back to what had happened on that day, four years ago.

◆ Is there a detective on the plane?

"What am I doing on a beautiful day like this?!"

The weather really didn't have much to do with anything, but...as I gazed through the window at the clouds, ten thousand meters up, in my second year of middle school, all I could do was curse my own fate.

The source of my worries was sitting in the luggage compartment above my seat. But there was no telling what would have happened to me if I'd refused a request from those *men in black*.

Man, if this isn't rotten luck, then what is it?

Just as I was lamenting my own fate—I heard *the sentence that would change my life.*

"Is there a detective on this plane?"

At first, I thought I'd misheard it.

After the second time, though, I accepted the reality: Some sort of situation that required a detective was unfolding on this plane.

I'll be honest with you, though. This was far from my first run-in with mysterious problems. I wasn't kidding when I said trouble always seems to find me.

That being the case, I thought I'd probably be able to duck-and-weave my way out of this one, too. If I closed my eyes, the storm would blow over before I knew it.

Naive, I know. I'll admit it.

However, what was different this time around…

What made me open my eyes was…

…first and foremost, the fact that *she* was in the seat next to mine.

"Yes, I'm a detective."

That was how we met: me, Kimihiko Kimizuka—and her, Siesta.

Her hair and eye color made it unlikely she was Japanese, and her symmetrical features were as delicate as spun glass. Her dress's unique design reminded me of a military uniform from some other country. All together, those elements gave her a beauty that was practically unreal.

This miracle of a girl had been right next to me, and up till that very moment, I hadn't even registered her existence. I couldn't believe myself—and I forgot everything, even the situation I was in.

"What's your name…?"

However, this was a fateful encounter of a different sort.

"Perfect timing. You—be my assistant."

"Huh?"

No sooner had she spoken than the girl caught my hand and stood up.

"This way, please!"

"We'll be right there."

The girl strode off, following the cabin attendant…and since she was pulling me by the hand, I followed her. Under the stunned, open-mouthed gazes of the other passengers, our weird procession advanced.

What is this? What's happening?

…Oh, right. A detective, huh?

The girl's vivid presence had almost erased it from my memory already—right now, something was happening on this plane, and a detective was needed to resolve it. And she'd called me…her assistant?

This beautiful girl who had me by the hand was a detective, and I was her assistant.

I'd been born as a magnet for unusual situations and had spent the past dozen or so years surviving all sorts of trouble, and even I was having a really hard time following this development.

The girl didn't notice my confusion and said, "Siesta." Just one word, and she didn't even look back as she said it. "That's my name."

"…Kinda weird one," I finally managed to say.

"It's a code name."

"A code name?"

"People do have those, usually."

"No they don't, usually." *They don't, do they? Usually?*

"Then what's your name?"

"Kimihiko…Kimizuka."

"I see. I'll call you 'Kimi,' then."

"…Is that a nickname?"

When I asked her that, for the first time, Siesta looked back at me.

"Good question. What do you think it is?"

The smile she flashed me was a hundred million watts of adorable.

But this was no time for romantic comedy shenanigans.

The cabin attendant led us to the cockpit, which was the worst possible place to have problems on a plane.

"I've brought a detective and the detective's assistant."

My title is spreading way too fast…

I didn't even have time to make a retort, though, as the situation was still evolving.

When the attendant knocked on the door, I heard an electronic beep, followed by a lock disengaging, and then the heavy door opened.

"Holy..." I couldn't believe my eyes.

Two men, the pilot and copilot, were sitting in the seats of the cramped cockpit.

The older one—probably the pilot—was gripping the control stick, his face ashen. The younger man, the copilot, was doubled over and unconscious—*while another man was sitting cross-legged on top of him.*

"Hey, you actually found a detective?"

The man had striking blond hair and emerald eyes.

He was speaking Japanese, but his features and the color of his skin suggested he was from northern Europe.

From his spot on top of the copilot's body, the man glanced coolly from my face to Siesta's and back.

"You're younger than I expected, but whatever. So. Which one's supposed to be the detective?" he asked mockingly.

Was he trying to intimidate us, to maintain as much of an advantage as he could?

He hardly needed to, though; we were already in deep shit. Even I hadn't run into a hijacker before, and my knees went weak despite my attempts to keep them steady.

"First of all, what's your name?" Siesta asked.

The pilot was still pale, the copilot was still unconscious, and the flight attendant was so sweaty that her makeup was running, but she was the one person who hadn't frozen up. Ignoring the incapacitated adults, this teenage girl barred the hijacker's way, all alone.

"Bat. It's a code name," the man said.

Siesta turned to me. "There, you see? Everybody has a code name."

"Look, I don't care!"

I seriously could not care less about that! This really isn't the time!

For some reason, Siesta looked a little proud of herself, but I made her face forward again, toward Bat the hijacker.

"I am Siesta, and this is my assistant, Watson. We grew up together on

Baker Street." She lied like it was nothing. Her nerves were way too steady. "Well, Bat? What are you trying to do? Why have you called me, *the ace detective*, here?"

Oh, right. Yeah.

Thanks to Siesta's carefree attitude, I'd almost forgotten the actual situation.

"Ha-ha, ha-ha! You're funny, girl. I like it; this might be fun."

Bat laughed, then spoke from his spot on top of the copilot.

"Deduce why I've hijacked this plane. If you get it right, I won't snap the pilot's neck."

In that moment—the lives of six hundred passengers and crew members were entrusted to the skill of a single detective.

◆ Hijacker vs. ace detective

"The reason you hijacked this plane?"

Siesta echoed his words, putting a finger to her delicate chin.

"You called me here just to make me deduce that?"

"Yeah, that's right. I wanted to play a little game. A high-stakes game with the lives of all six hundred passengers in the balance... Sound like fun?" Bat smirked, letting his gaze crawl all over us. Just looking at this guy made me feel sick. "All you two have to do to win is guess why I hijacked the plane. That's it."

"In other words, if we guess correctly, everyone's lives will be spared, and if we get it wrong, they die?"

"Right. Nice and simple."

"Yes, it is. If we fail, though, you'll meet the same fate we do." Siesta fixed piercing eyes on Bat.

"...True. If I'm on a plane that's going down, I've got no way to save myself."

"Meaning you don't value your life?"

"If I don't get my kicks somehow, I don't feel like I'm really alive, et cetera, et cetera."

"I see. You're terribly bored, then."

Siesta was surprisingly fearless as she spoke with the hijacker. It felt as if there were invisible blades hidden in their joking exchange.

Was this battle about to escalate…?

"Yeah, I'm bored. The boredom got so bad that I went and hijacked a flight in a distant foreign country."

"All right, then that's it."

However, in the next instant—

"You hijacked the plane because you were desperately bored."

—she gave her final answer.

Without so much as phoning a friend, Siesta played her hand.

"…Siesta, wait, just hang on a second. Are you serious?"

His motive for the hijacking was—boredom?

That couldn't be right. They'd just been teasing at this grand show-down between a hijacker and an ace detective; this was a punchline. We wouldn't get away with this. The lives of the six hundred people on this plane were riding on that answer, remember?

"Of course I'm serious. The man said so himself, didn't he? He was bored, so very bored that he hijacked the plane."

"…Yeah, but he was probably just messing with you, don't you think?"

"Oh? Then you're saying he lied?"

"Huh?"

Siesta's eyes turned from me to Bat. "The ace detective frightened him, and he accidentally let something slip. To cover for himself, he'll say it was a lie to force me to admit a loss and end the game. Thus, we can infer that he's a coward?"

As she spoke, she didn't show a flicker of fear.

"—Ha-ha. Ha-ha-ha. Ha-ha-ha-ha-ha! Amazing! Ahhh, well done. Brilliant. That courage of yours is really something." Bat started to laugh. It was quiet at first, but gradually, as if he couldn't fully contain it, he began to guffaw, holding his sides. "Ahhh, I can't believe it. That's just insane. Never thought someone would talk me into a corner like that. Well, you got me. I'm beat."

Hey, whoa, are you kidding me?

Had he genuinely hijacked the plane just because he was bored?

Or had Siesta's incredibly bold bluff wiped out his will to fight?

"That ended faster than I thought it would, but you win some, you lose some. I've already achieved my objective, so I'll bow out here."

Bat got down from the copilot's body and walked toward us.

"Ah, don't worry. *That one's* only unconscious, not dead. I'll probably get arrested once we reach the airport, but I haven't killed anybody. If I *move into the big house* for a while, they'll let me leave again eventually."

Sighing, Bat sauntered past us, heading back to the seat he'd occupied originally.

"All right, wake me up when we land. Oh, and the media'll be a pain in the ass, so get me a sweatshirt or something to hide my face, wouldja?"

Then, just as he was about to make his exit...

"My, you really are a liar." Siesta's words held no emotion whatsoever.

"...What are you talking about?" Bat stopped in his tracks.

"Oh, nothing really."

"—Listen here, Miss Detective. You're right. The real reason I tried to hijack this plane is something else. Out of consideration for your bravery, I'm pretending I lost for you, see? C'mon, don't make me say everything."

So that really was the case, huh?

I thought he'd backed down awfully fast, but apparently he just respected Siesta's recklessness.

If I'd said I wasn't interested in knowing the truth, I would've been lying, but we could have the police figure that out after the plane was safely on the ground.

Right now, the important thing was to make sure this guy didn't change his mind. *Let's just let him return to his seat without disturbing him.* That thought was why I was the assistant here.

"He's right, Siesta. He's responding like an adult, so let's take a page from his book and go back where we came fr—"

"No, that wasn't the lie I was talking about."

...Oh, I see.

I guess nobody who was capable of responding like an adult would be calling herself an ace detective in the first place.

"The part where you said you had no qualms about risking your own life in this hijacking. That was a lie, wasn't it? You were actually *scared of dying*, weren't you?" Siesta lit the fuse again.

"...What are you saying?" Bat still had his back to us, but he wasn't moving, and his voice was low.

"You backed down too fast."

"From what?"

"When you admitted I'd won. Japan has a reputation for airline security; there's no way a man who would hijack a Japanese plane all by himself, in this day and age, would withdraw so easily because of one girl."

...That had actually been bothering me as well.

For having prepared such a huge prop, he'd given up far too easily. I'd been trying to convince myself that we were just lucky, but...Siesta hadn't let it slip past her.

"You were probably executing this hijack on instructions from someone else. In addition, you yourself were ordered to crash and die with the plane. Am I wrong?"

"......"

His silence indicated that she wasn't.

"But you don't want to. You're actually afraid to die, so you used us to give yourself an excuse that would let you survive. Correct?"

A hijacker had been given orders to die by somebody else. He'd obeyed the order initially, but when it got down to the wire, he'd realized he valued his life.

Thus, he'd come up with the idea of calling a detective and staging a deduction game: By making us guess his reason for the hijack, then aborting the attempt, he'd saved his own life along with the lives of the passengers.

"*When we reach the airport, the cops will arrest me*," Bat had said, sighing— but that sigh had been one of relief, not regret.

If the hijack ended in failure, Bat would be killed by whoever had ordered it. Which was why he'd decided to have the Japanese police protect him until the storm blew over.

...Meaning it hadn't mattered what his reason was.

Siesta could have said anything—money, securing a prisoner's release, a diplomatic issue, or any other reason—and Bat would have thrown up a plausible smoke screen to convince her she'd guessed right. After all, the one who'd most wanted this hijack to fail was Bat himself.

…Hmm. But in that case…

"In that case, why did he go out of his way to play his game? If he started wanting to give up on the hijack, he could have just surrendered. He didn't have to pull something like this, did he?"

No need to go to the trouble of finding and summoning a detective. All he'd had to do was get off the plane on his own, then turn himself in.

"His pride probably wouldn't allow it," Siesta murmured. "You didn't want to lose by default. You wanted to fight and be defeated. Even if it was only an act."

Was that how it was?

The man stood there, with his back to us, and he didn't say a word.

Not a single word.

"Hey, tell me one thing before *the end*."

As Siesta and I started back to our seats, Bat stopped us.

"How did you know all that?"

Finally, having been soundly beaten by the ace detective, the villain of this story asked her why he'd lost.

"What gave it away? Was it really just because I backed down too fast, or—?"

"Haaah. That was a factor as well, but…" Sounding unenthused, Siesta turned around. "I already knew about you."

"…What do you mean?"

"I knew you'd be on this plane today and that you were planning to hijack it. I know about your companions who ordered you to do it. Everything."

…*Wait, what?*

Knowing all that, she'd boarded this flight anyway?

Had she known how all this would play out from the very beginning?

"First-rate detectives resolve incidents before they even occur, you see. I was just a bit late, since I let myself fall asleep." Siesta ran her fingers through her hair.

Is that where she got her code name? She doesn't look Hispanic.

"...I see. So that's what it was." With his back still turned to us, Bat responded to Siesta's explanation impassively. "Well, I really am glad I asked that one thing, just in case, before *the end*."

"Assistant, get down," Siesta murmured from beside me.

"The thing is, when first-rate agents find a young sprout, we mow it down before it can grow."

The moment Bat said that, or maybe the moment before, a powerful shock ran through me.

"Ow, ow, ow..."

The next thing I knew, I was on my butt on the floor. Had something— Had Siesta pushed me?

"Hey, Siesta, what the heck was... Huh?"

Siesta was right in front of me. Dark-red liquid was pulsing out of her shoulder and streaming down her clothes.

Beyond her, Bat was standing still, raking his hair up with his fingers— and from his head, or rather, *from his ear, he'd sprouted something like a tentacle with a razor-sharp tip.*

"Change of plans. I'll slaughter you and leave the rest."

◆ Mystery meets sci-fi/fantasy

"...Ghk."

"Siesta!" I ran to the fallen detective—fallen because she'd protected me.

"Rgh, I shouldn't have hired an assistant... You haven't been any use at all so far..."

"That's not fair at all! You're the one who press-ganged me, all right?!"

She's right about me being useless, though!

No, but this was no time to be having a petty argument.

"What is that thing...?"

The tentacle from Bat's right ear was twisting and writhing as if it had a mind of its own. It was a grotesque color, like what you'd get if you mixed dark green and purple. It seemed capable of stretching and contracting freely as well; there was no telling how wide its range was.

"He's a pseudohuman." Shakily, Siesta got to her feet, holding her wounded shoulder. "That man is a member of the *clandestine organization* SPES. They use powers beyond human understanding to create pseudohumans. They're not publicly known, but they're a threat to the world."

"Pseudohumans…? That's insane. Then he's— Bat isn't…?"

He's not human? She's saying he's a monster?

"With him, it's still only his ear. He merely stole a prototype and forcibly attached it to himself. Basically, he's a half pseudohuman."

"Siesta, how do you know all this…?"

"Then, because he'd betrayed the organization, he was assigned this task as punishment."

"I asked you a question, Siesta! How do you know this stuff?!"

Don't tell me she's from that other group, too?

However, Bat's deep voice erased that doubt.

"You know your stuff, huh?! In that case, taking your corpse back to them as a little memento would be a better plan!"

The tentacle streaked toward us again.

"Hang on, assistant."

"Huh? …Whoa!"

I flew through the air—or rather, Siesta had hugged me to her and leaped out of the way.

Her snow-white hair stung my cheek.

Her name was Siesta, a nap taken during the daytime—and the sight really did seem as surreal as a *daydream.*

"Are *you* human?"

"Are you stupid, Kimi? Do I look like a monster?"

"I'm just saying I wouldn't be surprised if you were."

"…I'd bet anything you don't have a girlfriend, Kimi."

But this wasn't the time for a dumb conversation.

With six hundred passengers on the plane, of course people had noticed the racket.

"H-hey! Wh-wh-what the hell is that?!"

"Eeeeeeeeeeeeeeeeeeeeeeeeeeeeek!"

It started with the people who'd come up here to see what was going on, and a wave of screams and angry yelling began filling the plane.

"L-ladies and gentlemen! Please remain calm!"

The cabin attendant, whose makeup was completely ruined by now, hastily went to soothe the passengers. But the plane was already in pandemonium.

"Argh, if this is how it's gonna be, I don't even care," Bat said. "I'll just kill every human I don't need."

"—! Wait, just think about this! If you do that, the plane will crash, and you'll die, too!" I shouted.

"Ha! I'll let the pilot live. Wait, who are you again?"

"I'm the ace detective's assistant!"

Goddammit, now she's got me saying it. Behold the power of conditioning.

"My, you called me an ace detective. What a model apprentice."

"I just said what sounded good. Also, I'm your assistant, not your apprentice."

Argh, really? I did it again. Damn, she's good.

"Seriously, though, what the heck is that thing?" I asked. "You said 'pseudohuman' like it was nothing, but…"

I was hanging on to Siesta as we evaded Bat's attacks.

"Pseudohumans are monsters created around a core consisting of *a certain object.* This one fights with his ear, but there are loads of others who fight with their eyes or nose or teeth."

"—You fight these monsters, Siesta?"

"Yes, although this is the first time I've ended up in actual combat with one. Kimi, you know nothing about the world, do you?"

"Hey, no law-abiding middle schooler would know that much about the underworld."

"Perhaps, but you're a middle schooler flying across the ocean with a mysterious attaché case."

"Wait, how much do you know?!"

She'd even had her eye on me?

Plus, that attaché case has nothing to do with this business, does it? I swear, I genuinely don't know anything, all right?

"What are these jokers even after anyway? Were they planning to use the hijacking to declare war on Japan or something?"

"In Latin, the word *SPES* means 'hope'—and their goal is to grant 'salvation.'" As Siesta explained, she took a great leap, still holding me.

"Sounds like some sketchy religion..."

In the next instant, Bat's sharp tentacle plunged into the floor where we'd been just a moment ago.

We were flying at ten thousand meters. If he put a hole in the body of the plane, this story was over.

"I can't believe a threat this huge to us was hiding out in Japan!" Bat complained.

"Any detective worth her salt works in secret. As a matter of fact, none of your companions even knew I existed, did they?" Siesta taunted.

She was projecting an aura of cool composure, but as close as we were, I could tell from the way she was breathing that she wasn't in good shape.

She'd burned through quite a lot of her energy. That was only natural. She was fighting while protecting me, and I was deadweight.

"Ha-ha! In that case, all your sneaky secrets are gonna be pointless after today."

"Oh? But you can't go back to your organization, remember? You won't be able to tip them off."

"Well, I wouldn't be so sure about that. If I bribe them with information about you, even that short-tempered bunch may have a change of heart."

"You sure it'll be that easy?"

"Ha! You talk like you know."

Once again, like a flying snake, the sharp, writhing tentacle darted toward Siesta.

We were on an airplane, with no possible access to any effective weapons, which meant we had to stay on the defense. This was a battle of attrition that we were going to lose.

"What's the matter? You're breathing pretty hard."

"...I was being careful to hide that." For the first time, Siesta's expression clouded over slightly.

"Ha-ha, these ears are custom-made. The acoustic cells concentrated in the tip of this tentacle *can even pick out the heartbeat of someone a hundred kilometers away.*"

"...I should've gathered more intel. I suppose I really can't disguise my heart rate."

Even if she was an ace detective, she wasn't all-knowing. Sweat broke out on Siesta's forehead.

Right now, though, there was nothing I could do.

"If I just had a weapon or something..."

Obviously, but we were ten thousand meters up.

All we had available was what was already here, and security wouldn't even allow a knife onto a plane. None of the passengers could possibly have anything resembling a weapon in their luggage...

No. *There was one person.*

"Siesta, buy me thirty seconds."

"Assistant?"

"I've got an idea."

Even at a time like this—or maybe because it was a time like this—my mind was running on all cylinders.

I've been getting dragged into trouble since I was born. Over the course of my life, I've survived more ugly situations than I've eaten slices of bread. My past experience was telling me this hunch had to be the best solution.

"All right. You haven't been doing anything, so no complaints here."

"Just let me have my moment, wouldja?!"

As we lobbed nonsense at each other, I ran hell-for-leather back to my seat.

"Move it, move it! Out of the way!"

Shoving my way through the passengers, who were clogging the aisles in confusion, I made it to my seat—and hauled *that attaché case* out of the overhead luggage compartment.

Naturally, I had no idea what was in it. I didn't know whether it would be useful in this situation. Was the cat in the box alive or dead?

However, during the carry-on luggage inspection at the airport, I'd noticed *the personnel exchanging looks.*

I'd been concerned about the level of Japanese airport security...but thanks to that, I could take this gamble.

"Siesta! Catch!"

Running back would take too long; I threw the ridiculously big silver attaché case toward the battlefield with all my might.

"Ghk! That's not gonna happen!" Instead of targeting the bloodied Siesta this time, Bat redirected the tentacle and smashed the attaché case—but as a result, the *contents* ended up right in Siesta's hands.

And then—Siesta *shot the tentacle with her newly acquired musket.*

"Gwaaaaaaaaaaaaaaaaaaaaaaaaaargh!"

My bet had paid off.

Spraying a grotesque fluid around, the tentacle slithered back into Bat's ear.

Siesta didn't stop there. She closed the distance between herself and Bat all at once, wrestled him to the floor, shoved the gun against his throat, and—

"Bang!"

—mimicked the sound of a gunshot.

Bat was nonplussed, but Siesta was calm and composed. "There," she said. "As of now, you're dead."

Bat shot her a look, obviously wondering what she was talking about.

I didn't know what was going on here, either. So she wasn't going to finish him off...?

"Now your comrades won't come after you. After all, you're only a corpse."

"...You little rat. Are you mocking me?" Bat snarled as she withdrew the gun.

"Well, you don't want to die, correct?"

"...Ha! After this, that's off the table. I was going to use you as bait, and you beat me. They'll bump me off for sure."

"You don't have to worry. I'll have the media report that you died here."

"Who exactly are you...?"

"I'll also have the Japanese police shelter you. It's all right. I have a reliable connection."

Bat laughed with disbelief... Frankly, I wanted to do the same.

What on earth was this girl? The word *detective* was kind of underplaying this, I thought.

"If you don't kill me here, you'll regret it."

"Why?"

"I'm vindictive. I swear I'll get you back for making a fool of me."

"You won't be able to." Siesta got up, releasing Bat. "The red bullet I shot into you a minute ago was made from my blood, you see? Anyone who's hit with that blood becomes absolutely unable to defy their master. Meaning, *your tentacle will never be able to attack me again.*"

"...How the hell does that work?"

"Trade secret."

"Did somebody hire you for this, too?"

Siesta smiled faintly.

"No—I was born to be an ace detective. It's how I'm wired."

I see. Apparently, there are people in the world with even worse DNA than mine.

Still, that aside...

"Sorry to interrupt while you're putting a neat bow on everything, Siesta, but..."

I had major questions about something in that conversation.

"That 'red bullet' you mentioned—where did you find that sort of time?"

I'd thrown the attaché case, Bat had destroyed it...and Siesta had caught the long-barreled gun as it fell, then fired at the tentacle. Was she saying she'd had time to make such a special bullet in those scant few seconds?

No, that really wasn't possible.

Meaning the work had to have been done on the bullet *already*...and Siesta had to have known about it. I had a bad feeling about this.

Nonchalant as ever, Siesta said, "I was the one who told them to have you bring that attaché case onto the plane in the first place."

"So you were pulling my strings all along?!"

And that was how our dazzling three-year adventure began.

◆ Even now, I remember

"That was how I met Bat—and the former ace detective."

Lengthy as it was, I'd finally filled Natsunagi in on the old memory Bat and I shared. If I was telling stories from four years ago, there was no way to avoid the topic of my former partner.

It had been a long time since I'd talked about her, and while not all the memories were good—for reasons incomprehensible to me—they put a smile on my face.

"I see... Okay. I understand your story, but, uh," Natsunagi said, surreptitiously sidling back, "doesn't that mean he's super-dangerous?"

She backed up all the way to the opposite wall, trying to put some distance between herself and Bat.

"Ah, hmm, well."

"Is that all you have to say? You're a pretty dangerous character yourself, Kimizuka."

Come to think of it, I hadn't filled Natsunagi in on my issues with getting dragged into stuff...but she really should have caught on back when she found out I knew people on the police force and in prison.

"Also, I don't want a guy like him listening to my heart..."

Well, yes, she had a point. Having that nasty tentacle on her chest could be a devastatingly traumatic experience for an adolescent girl. I wouldn't want it happening to me, either.

"No, no. I can hear your heart just fine from here—and in fact, sweetheart, I've already identified it."

Bat guessed what Natsunagi and I were worried about and headed us off.

...But what had he said just now? Did he mean he already had an idea of who Natsunagi's donor was?

"Bat, are you saying you've met the owner of Natsunagi's heart?"

"Yeah. That was the point of that old story."

It was?

The guy was making as little sense as ever. What could that story have to do with Natsunagi's heart? He wasn't saying her donor had been in the story, on that plane four years ago, was he?

"—Oh."

Behind me, Natsunagi murmured quietly.

"What is it? Did you figure something out?"

"...Well, it's just...I thought it was strange."

If we were talking "strange," Natsunagi had been strange from the moment I met her...but cracking a joke right now would have felt wrong.

"You see, I'm not actually the type who does *that sort of thing*."

"What are you talking about, Natsunagi? You've been acting kind of weird for a while now."

"You're right. I am weird. Sometimes I don't understand why I do certain things—it's like I stop being myself." Natsunagi's usual composure had vanished, and she was hugging her shoulders slightly. "I mean, I'm not the type who'd do *a thing like that* to a boy I'd just met."

Was she talking about what had happened in the classroom the previous day? That she wasn't actually that audacious?

In that case, what had pushed her to do it? Well, I had talked to her about something similar the day before.

"Memory transference—that's what you said, Kimizuka. Remember? That means I wasn't the one who did that. I bet the owner of this heart made me do it."

By that logic, before they died, Natsunagi's donor *could* do "that sort of thing."

Someone who didn't care about shame or their reputation or the means, as long as it was for an end they believed was right.

I knew just one person who could pull off such a trick.

And that person—had died exactly a year ago.

...No. Don't tell me.

A coincidence like that would never happen. That's just ludicrous.

Cold sweat broke out on my forehead. My hands and feet grew numb, and my teeth chattered.

Stop it. Please stop.

Don't follow me anymore.

I'm not your partner now.

Isn't that right?

You're already dead, aren't you?

"Denial isn't a good look for you, Watson."

When I looked up, Bat was gazing at me with those cloudy eyes. Like he was telling me not to close mine.

"This is the answer."

The sharp tentacle I'd seen that day emerged from Bat's ear. Still that grotesque shade, as if someone had mixed dozens of paint colors together, and that sickening slug-like way of moving.

"Don't do it, Bat."

"Do what?"

"If you kill someone, you'll hang for it."

"Right. *If*," Bat said. "But you know *I can't kill her* with this, don't you?"

"Stop!"

The tentacle sharpened into a spike, took aim at Natsunagi's heart, and—a few centimeters before it touched her, *the tip crumbled away*.

That phenomenon triggered a memory for me.

It was something a certain someone had said, four years ago:

"Your tentacle will never be able to attack me again."

Anyone who was hit with that blood became absolutely unable to defy their master, she'd said.

Bat's tentacle hadn't been able to attack Natsunagi...or to be precise, the heart that was inside her. That meant—

"Siesta, is it you?"

The nostalgia I'd felt in that sunset classroom, when Natsunagi had held me in her arms—the trigger had been the heartbeat of my worst and dearest former partner. I'd met her again for the first time in a year.

"The moment you walked in, I had assumed that girl was your partner."

Now that he mentioned it, when we'd shown up, Bat had gotten oddly nostalgic... Had it been because he'd heard the sound of his mortal enemy's heart?

Bat couldn't see, so when he'd heard that heartbeat, he'd mistaken Natsunagi for Siesta. Was that why our conversation hadn't gelled at the beginning?

"When did that ace detective die?" Bat asked, narrowing his eyes.

"...A year ago. On a faraway island, in a distant ocean."

"I see. Even if she was an enemy, that's a shame."

"Yeah. Out of nowhere, just like that, it was over."

"'Just like that'? Don't be an idiot. Even after she died, the detective has come back to you."

For a moment, Bat's words made my chest feel tight.

Siesta had come back to me—yeah. That would be poetic, wouldn't it? If it was true.

She'd be the last person to do a thing like that, though. She was a logical ace detective—this theory was too convenient, too trite, too emotional.

...Besides, I'd been a lousy assistant.

Yeah, I admit it. I'd complained constantly... But really, I knew how incredible Siesta was and how much I was her polar opposite.

I was just her shadow, a dark shape following a beautiful girl dancing as lightly as a dream in the bright sunlight.

That's why... That's why I knew saying that Siesta had come back to me definitely wasn't right.

After all, she would have forgotten me long before now.

"It's a coincidence," I murmured, but I wasn't really talking to Bat. It was a reminder to myself. "Running into Natsunagi, and her having Siesta's heart, is all just—"

That was when Natsunagi slapped me across the face.

"...Did the heart's owner make you do that, too?" I asked.

"No!"

When I looked at her, she was crying. "I did that on my own! I hit you because I wanted to!"

Her eyes were red, her face was crumpled, and she erupted at the top of her lungs.

"Kimizuka, I dare you to say that one more time! This is coincidence? This reunion is *coincidence*?! Come on! Why are you being so irresponsible and fatalistic? This is a reunion; don't brush it off! These are feelings! You were together for three years, and she wants to be with you even after she died! That's the only wish this little heart has! I've been— This heart has been looking for you this whole time, Kimihiko Kimizuka! So it could see you again… Just so it could see you! And then you try to shut it down with a word like *coincidence*! These feelings *matter*!"

The next thing I knew, I'd run to her and pulled her slim body into my arms.

I understand. I see it now.

It was like I'd said—the heart inside Natsunagi was searching for someone.

"X," the person Natsunagi had been trying to find for the past year, that Siesta had been trying to find, was…me.

Siesta had wanted to see me?

"Are you there?" I asked.

There was no answer. Of course there wasn't.

The detective was already dead.

But…

"It's been a long time, Siesta."

…the warmth of this chest was definitely hers.

"Actually, I had a ton of things I wanted to say to you."

How hard do you think life was for me after I became your assistant?

I was forced to smuggle a gun, and we wound up in a paranormal battle with a shadowy organization, and our names spread through underworld society, and I ended up having to travel the world with you for three whole years while fleeing from our pursuers; we were flat broke and living hand to mouth while fighting a bunch of pseudohumans,

sleeping out in the open during hurricanes, and sometimes on days when we won big at a casino, we'd jump on the bed at a resort hotel together, and then the next day, we'd be penniless again. We traveled across deserts, and through jungles, and over mountains and oceans, and then, and then—

"—Why'd you go and die first, you moron?"

I didn't have feelings for you or anything.
It was the same for you, wasn't it?
You and I weren't lovers, and I'm sure we weren't even really friends.
We were detective and assistant—just business partners, in an odd way.
But... But still...
You recruited me, remember? You can't just die and leave me after that. At least tell me good-bye before you go.
"Is that why you came back?"
To say good-bye?
Or maybe...

"I'm looking forward to continuing this relationship."

As Natsunagi spoke, she smoothly stepped away from me.
Her face was— No, I really must have been imagining it that time.
But I could almost see a faintly familiar hundred-million-watt smile.

◆ The detective is already dead

After that, Ms. Fuubi came to pick us up, and Natsunagi and I followed her out of the prison.
"Did you get to ask your questions?" Hands on the police car's steering wheel, Ms. Fuubi directed the question at us, in the back seat.
"...Yes, more or less."
Natsunagi's eyes were still red, and I answered for her.
"Wow. His lips have gotten surprisingly loose."

"It probably depends on the topic. He won't say a word about *that other subject*, will he?"

"That other subject" was why Siesta had captured Bat alive on that plane. Ms. Fuubi had taken him into custody after that, but even four years later, she apparently hadn't managed to get any significant information out of him.

Just so you know, ever since Siesta's death, we'd been in a cease-fire with SPES. Or to be more accurate, they'd stopped going out of their way to fight me. I guess it means I was only ever the ace detective's flunky as far as they were concerned. Too bad.

"Well, I'm glad you two got what you wanted anyway. You'd better be damn grateful to me."

Ms. Fuubi seemed to have forgotten that we had just followed her because she had business here. Either way, I really was damn grateful.

There was just one thing, though. A question I couldn't get out of my mind. "You knew everything to begin with, didn't you, Ms. Fuubi?"

"What're you talking about?"

"About who Natsunagi's heart belonged to."

"What makes you think that?"

"That's a good question, and I'm not sure how to answer it. Just a vague hunch."

I had nothing solid to base it on. But after she'd brought us right to the man we needed to see, I couldn't believe that it meant nothing.

And if so, then maybe Ms. Fuubi's objective was—

"Natsunagi."

I was positive this was something I needed to say, right now.

Still facing forward, I spoke to the girl sitting next to me.

"No matter who that heart belongs to, it's okay for you to live your own life. You don't have to replace anyone."

I saw Ms. Fuubi's reflection deflate in the rearview mirror.

Sorry, but I'll leave smiting the pseudohumans to you people. I'm not going to drag Natsunagi into this. I won't let you make her Siesta's replacement.

"Kimizuka..."

When I glanced to the side, Natsunagi was gazing at me, stunned.

"What's wrong?"

"...Nothing."

Before long, she shook her head slightly.

"—Thanks!"

She smiled, like a flower bursting into bloom.

"Ahhh, well, that was a lot."

After Ms. Fuubi had dropped us off outside the station, I stretched.

I swear. My first proper job in a year...and to make matters worse, it unexpectedly dredged up a bunch of past trauma and random other stuff. I felt like I'd just gotten the beating of my life.

"Is it my fault?" Natsunagi peered into my face, unusually apologetic.

"I didn't say that. As a matter of fact, I'm grateful to you."

"Huh...?" Her already large eyes grew even wider.

"Thanks to you, well, uh..."

Hmm. Even I couldn't put it into words very well. But when I met Natsunagi, then ended up facing my past again...

"I started thinking it wasn't okay to stay like this."

Or at least, I think I did. I can't say for sure just yet.

"If so, then I—" Natsunagi bit her lip. She seemed to be thinking hard.

What was it? Was she still worried about something?

I considered asking, but then—

"Thanks for today."

—I turned to go, pretending I hadn't noticed anything.

After all, I'd already taken care of Natsunagi's request.

There was no need for me to be involved with her anymore. We should cut ties here and now.

Needless to say, Natsunagi and I weren't lovers, and I'm sure we weren't even really friends.

Detective (stand-in) and client—that was all our relationship was. Now that the request was cleared up, we had no relationship at all.

Which meant I needed to leave Natsunagi quickly.

She'd managed to get a new life. That meant *she shouldn't be bound by Siesta.*

And since I could become a trigger that made her think about Siesta, *she shouldn't get involved with me, either.*

"See you around." With those thoughts in my mind, I took a step toward the station's ticket gate—

"Wait."

—or tried to, until slim fingers caught my right hand.

"...What's the matter, Natsunagi?"

"No, um..."

Her fingers were still closed around mine. Her eyes were on the ground; she was opening her mouth as if she wanted to say something, then closing it again.

I knew what she wanted to say, *what she was trying to be kind enough to say.*

But I couldn't let her.

This was her life. I couldn't make her shoulder someone else's burden.

Over our silent heads, an idol song was blaring from the huge screen outside the station. It was probably some sort of promo video. A middle school girl was singing a pop song, winking flirtatiously at the camera. It was also making the silence about 20 percent more awkward.

"If you don't have anything to say, I'm leaving."

"...You're kind of a jerk, Kimizuka." That was the third time she'd said that to me.

Yeah, I know. Something really glitched out when my personality was created. Sorry about that.

Leaving Natsunagi behind, I made another attempt to head for the ticket gate, when—

"Excuse me!"

—somebody else showed up and stopped me again.

I glanced to the side. Natsunagi was there. She'd tilted her head in confusion. It hadn't been her this time.

I looked down slightly, and then the owner of the voice came into view.

It was a middle school girl. Her face was half-hidden by a hood, but the eye that peeked out at me was shining a bit too brightly, and the aura around her couldn't possibly belong to an ordinary person.

Actually, I got the feeling I'd seen her somewhere before...

Natsunagi and I both looked waaay up, and a very familiar-looking idol was still singing her song on the giant screen.

"Um, actually, I'm an idol singer."

Hey, come on, I just finished a job. Why are clients showing up back-to-back like this? ...Wait, if there is a reason...

I looked over at Natsunagi—at her heart.

As it turned out, my sixth sense was right on the money.

"I have a problem I'd like an ace detective to solve!"

Goddammit. So I have to explain this whole thing again?

"Sorry, I'm not actually a detective..."

But then—

"Yes, I'm sorry; the slacker here is *only an assistant.*"

—Natsunagi sent me a quiet, significant look. She was telling me, *This is the path I've chosen.*

"Huh? Then..."

"It's all right, though."

Natsunagi spoke to the bewildered idol.

To her new client.

"If you need a detective, you've found one. I'm the ace detective—Nagisa Natsunagi."

The detective is already dead.

But her last wish will never die.

A girl's monologue 1

I feel like I've been looking for someone for ages, before I even knew what I was doing. But really, it's only been about a year...and to be honest, I feel like my "identity," if that's the word for it, was established only recently.

No, hold on. Don't snark at me just yet.

Ever since I was little, I was sick and bedridden. I didn't really need a sense of self...well, to be more accurate, I'm sure I was trying hard not to have one.

I wanted to pull on a pair of running shoes and sprint around a track. I wanted to walk home from school with a big group of friends and stop for bubble tea together.

That was never an option, though.

And if wishing wouldn't make it happen, then it was better not to wish at all. With that in mind, I constantly warned myself *not to develop a self.*

I don't have many old memories, really. Maybe some vague glimpses of being tucked into a small bed in a small room, but other than that, I can't remember much. When I try, my head just starts to hurt—

But it was fine. Or that's what I told myself.

And then one day, I developed a wish I desperately wanted to fulfill.

This chest, this heart, was screaming that it wanted to see someone.

What should I do?

I'd never wished for anything. I'd never thought I would get a chance to accomplish anything.

What could I do? Was I capable of granting this heart's wish?

—The next thing I knew, I'd broken into a run.

Now, I had legs that could hit the asphalt and shove it away from me. I had a storm of emotions that had been building for eighteen years. As long as I had those, I was invincible.

"You're the ace detective?"

And then the hope I'd finally found was listless, unambitious, and resigned. He'd given up on almost everything. He reminded me of who I used to be.

That meant I couldn't just leave him like that. I ended up telling him off, and I accidentally let him see me cry. I…really didn't mean for any of that to happen.

And then I made another blunder and let him save me again.

"No matter who that heart belongs to, it's okay for you to live your own life, Natsunagi."

That was what he told me.
And so, I'm sure…
…today, here and now, my life is beginning again.

One day, two years ago

"Hmm-hmm, hmm-hmmmm."

Even under a blazing sun, as we walked through a dense, overgrown forest, my partner was humming cheerfully.

"You're in an awfully good mood, Siesta."

We were traveling again today, in pursuit of—or possibly being pursued by—SPES. Nevertheless, it seemed the girl who called herself an ace detective wasn't feeling the tension at all.

"Well, any adult ought to know how to put herself in a good mood," Siesta said, breaking off mid-hum.

Uh, you're not actually an adult yet. I almost said it, but...I didn't actually know how old she was. Apparently, a true ace detective doesn't reveal her identity that easily. I mean, she still hadn't even told me her real name.

"What song was that?" I asked. Surely she'd tell me that, at least.

"It's an idol song from Japón."

"'Japón'? What country are you from?"

Well, Siesta may not be Japanese at all.

"Still, I didn't know someone like you would be into idols."

"Any detective worthy of the name has to be able to sing an idol's popular songs, at least."

"I've said this before: I really don't get your concept of detectives."

Hi, everybody! I'm a chart-topping ace detective! I sing, I dance, and sometimes I fight pseudohumans!

...That would break my brain.

"That's not what I meant. What I'm saying is that, if you want to become a detective, you have to see more of life. Literally. Of the five human senses, sight and hearing are especially important."

See more of life…? Does she mean to constantly pay attention to the world around me? And then to collect information using my eyes and ears? Okay, got it.

"Well, I've got no plans to become a detective, so not like I need to know any of that."

"Haaah. You really aren't cute at all."

Shove it. I don't need your pity, either.

"I suppose you're right. You really won't ever be a detective."

"Yeah, see?"

"Yes. I'm sure you'll always be *somebody's assistant* instead."

"…Hmm? Uh, yeah."

For some reason, Siesta's eyes turned vaguely lonely. However, that only lasted a moment before her usual cool expression returned. "Now, then! We've almost reached our destination." She pointed at a huge mansion that looked like an old castle.

"You really think Medusa is there?"

Medusa—a monster said to turn anyone who saw her eyes into stone. We'd overheard a dubious rumor that this mansion was haunted by that monster, so we were checking into it.

"I couldn't say. If such a being really exists, it'll be part of the executive ranks of SPES, but…"

"Well, we won't know until we see it."

I'd gotten tired of sighing and rolling my eyes, so I gave a huge yawn instead…and Siesta, who was walking beside me, took a moment to study me.

"What?" I said.

"…No. I was just thinking you'd gotten pretty used to all this."

"Not by choice."

Whistling, we headed toward the European-style mansion, with a flock of crows wheeling overhead.

"Well, well! Once again, thank you for coming all this way."

Siesta and I were seated in chairs facing the old master of the mansion, who wore a gentle smile.

"It must have been hot outside. I must apologize; I'm afraid the air-conditioning isn't working at the moment."

"No, don't worry about it."

Siesta wasn't sweating the tiniest bit, from the heat or from nerves. She was as formidable as ever. Personally, I was silently grousing that if he thought it was worth an apology, he could at least open a window.

...Still, we could probably count ourselves lucky that the worst-case scenario we'd been anticipating hadn't actually happened.

Frankly, we'd assumed the fighting might start the moment we knocked on the door—but instead, we'd been met with an unexpected welcome. As you might have guessed from the earlier conversation, Siesta and I said we'd come because of that rumor, and the man had introduced himself as the mansion's master and gladly invited us in.

He'd shown us into the living room, and we'd gotten down to business right away, hoping to learn the truth of the "Medusa."

"In that case, am I to assume you are aware of that particular rumor, sir?"

As Siesta asked her question, both her expression and posture were resolute.

"Yes, indeed I am. They speak of a Medusa who turns visitor after visitor here into stone... I believe they are speaking of my daughter. Adopted daughter, to be precise; we are not related by blood." As he spoke, the man's expression turned grim.

"You're not telling us she's really—?!"

"No, it's a misunderstanding!" The man rose to his feet, agitated by my question. "Two years ago, my daughter met with an accident. Fortunately, her life was spared, but...only her life!"

"—A persistent vegetative state," Siesta supplied.

The man nodded, looking anguished. "My daughter is unconscious and incapable of moving. She does nothing but blink and breathe. In a way, she *is* stone! They have it the wrong way around! My daughter is not Medusa. She is a victim, turned to stone *by* that mythical monster!"

"Then you're saying that information was distorted, and that's the rumor that spread?" I said.

"I suppose that is the only explanation." The man nodded weakly, agreeing with my guess. After that, for a little while, silence fell in the room. "...Ah, I beg your pardon. What a disgrace; I let myself go to pieces. It really is rather humid, isn't it? I'll go get you something cold to drink."

Finally, pulling himself together, the master withdrew for a moment.

"Sounds like we struck out here."

Apparently, SPES wasn't involved in this incident. Heck, it wasn't even an incident. Well, if extra trouble wasn't going to break out, I wasn't about to complain. We'd just accept those cold drinks, then head back. The heat was really getting to me now, so I undid a couple of shirt buttons.

"Why don't you strip, too?" I teased.

"Are you stupid, Kimi?"

"Ow!"

Still expressionless, Siesta stomped on my foot, hard. *At least look at me, wouldja?*

"My apologies for the wait." The man returned, carrying a tray with glasses on it. As I moved to take one—

"Ow!!!"

—Siesta stomped on my foot again, and I pitched forward violently. Naturally, the contents of the glasses splashed everywhere, soaking everything.

"Siesta, you little—!"

"That was for sexually harassing me."

"But you already stomped on me for that."

Siesta didn't even seem to hear my complaint. She went over to the man, whose clothes had gotten wet from the spill, and began to dry them with her handkerchief.

"I'm terribly sorry. My assistant has made an awful blunder."

What, like that was my fault? This is so unfair...

"Ha-ha, it's no trouble... But if I could burden you, would you come to meet my daughter? We don't often have guests, and I'm sure she'll be delighted."

"Yes, of course."

Siesta gave him her very best smile.

"Mary, look. You have guests."

The mansion's master had led us to a third-floor room, where the girl,

Mary, lay in a canopy bed. She was delicate, with bright-blond hair, and her mechanically blinking eyes were jade green. I'd say she was as lovely as a doll—but she wasn't. She was on a ventilator, desperately struggling to live. Mary was no doll.

Feeling an uncomfortable sense of regret, I looked away, leaving the situation in Siesta's hands. Maybe it was the guilt, but it felt a little hard to breathe.

"Oh, my poor Mary. You're so very beautiful, and yet the people outside the forest call you a monster. It's too much to bear."

The man buried his face in his hands, lamenting the tragedy that had befallen his daughter.

...Oh. That could be why he'd welcomed us. An ace detective would understand that his daughter was no Medusa, no monster. He thought we'd set the record straight.

"Yes," I said, "we'll be sure to tell the people outside the forest that the rumor's not—"

I tried to walk over to the man—but the next thing I knew, the floor was right in front of my face.

...*The floor? Did I fall? Why?*

For some reason, my body felt weak.

"It's all right, Mary. I'm making more friends for you now."

...What was he saying?

Shifting my head, which could still move a little, I looked up at the old man.

The guy was smiling.

"Ha-ha, ha-ha-ha. It's all right; you don't have to be frightened. It won't hurt. There's nothing to fear." He took a syringe out of the pocket of his trousers and jabbed the needle into—his own right arm. I had no idea what he was thinking.

"Did you think I was going to stab you? Ha-ha. This is an antidote. After all, the poison's been in this room all along."

Wh...what? So the reason I'm going numb is...

"Before long, your bodies will cease all physical activity. You'll end up just like Mary—unable to move a step, yet unable to die. You will suffer for eternity!"

...I...see. So that's why all the windows were closed... Plus, he'd said the only thing Mary could do was breathe on her own. He'd put her on a ventilator anyway, to protect her from the poison. I should've noticed that sooner.

"Now, very soon, both you and the ace detective over there will become Mary's companions...her...companions..."

That was when an abrupt change came over the man. His eyes flew open as if something had startled him...and then his knees buckled and sent him to the floor, face-first, just the way I had.

"Wh-why...?"

As he murmured in despair, the person who came over to him...was exactly who you're thinking.

"Behave."

Restraining the man with the handcuffs she always carried, she took the musket she'd been hiding behind her back and shattered the window...which allowed the poison to diffuse outside.

Once she'd taken care of that, the ace detective finally turned around and spoke to her assistant crawling across the floor.

"Are you stupid, Kimi?"

I see. No wonder she'd stomped on my foot twice.

"So you'd already figured out what he was after."

We were on our way back from the mansion, after we'd filed all the proper reports and paperwork and everything had been dealt with. My body was still numb, so Sierra was carrying me piggyback.

"Mm-hmm. I can't believe you almost accepted that drink; it was so obvious."

"Look, I said I was sorry..."

The drinks had probably been poisoned as well. Siesta had stomped on my foot to protect me... Wasn't there a kinder, gentler way to do it?

"Back then... While you were using that handkerchief to dry off his clothes, you switched out the syringe with the antidote?"

"Exactly. Then I used it, so I was fine."

As always, she'd just done what she wanted. She took care of jobs on her own, without consulting anybody else. Although the fact that I couldn't keep up with her might be part of the problem.

"Of course, all of that was merely circumstantial evidence. I wasn't certain until I saw Mary's eyes."

"Her eyes? But wasn't she unconscious?"

"No, she was blinking desperately, pleading with us. That motion was completely regular, not automatic… There was a will behind it. I'm sure she was trying to tell us about her adoptive father's misdeeds."

So in the grip of his insanity, the man hadn't noticed his own daughter's signal. That thought struck me as pathetic… Or maybe just sad.

"Good job spotting that."

"Are you stupid, Kimi?"

"That's the third time today. This is so unfair…"

Well, today I had no excuses to give.

"Did you forget what I said on the way to that mansion? About seeing more of the world and the importance of honing your sight and hearing? You should be more sensitive to where others are looking, too."

"I see. That's why you're the ace detective."

In terms of self-defense, I guess that's a skill I might need later on.

"Hey, Siesta."

"Hmm?"

So first off, I'd start by doing as Siesta said and learn more about the world. "Would you tell me the name of the idol whose song you were humming today?"

I could only see her face in profile, but she looked satisfied.

"Her name is—"

Chapter 2

◆ That's right—she's the self-proclaimed "cutest idol"

"—My name is Yui Saikawa! I'm an idol singer!"

It was just one damn thing after another.

Detectives are magnets for problems that need solving.

It was evening on a weekend, in front of a train station. Apparently having heard the rumors about me, a new client introduced herself to Natsunagi and me.

Yui Saikawa was a singing, dancing middle school idol who was currently attracting massive amounts of attention in Japan.

From what I'd heard, she'd made her professional debut in sixth grade. Ever since then, people of all ages and genders had loved her for her exceptional gifts in singing and dance, and especially for her adorable face. Her album sales always topped the weekly charts, and thanks to her looks, you could catch her frequently on magazine covers and in TV commercials.

…Still. Yui Saikawa, huh?

Hey, Siesta. Is this another coincidence? Or—

Even so, no one but Siesta herself could know about that conflict.

Yui Saikawa sucked in a deep breath, then shouted at Natsunagi and me:

"I want you to stop the theft of a sapphire that's worth three billion yen!"

★ ★ ★

I know I just said this, but this was a weekend evening in front of a train station.

I'm pretty sure you can imagine what the crowds were like. If a middle school girl started yelling about a three-billion-yen sapphire getting stolen there, it was perfectly natural for all those eyes to end up on her.

Consequently, it's fair to say what I did next was also perfectly natural.

"Yes, okay, shut up a second."

I turned to this active idol, a middle school girl I'd only just met—and smacked both my hands over her mouth.

"Mmph! Mmmmmmmmrrgh! Mmmmmmmmmmmmmmmmmph!"

"Okay, come on. Easy, easy."

As Saikawa struggled and kicked, I wrapped my arm around her, desperately trying to muffle her shouts.

After all, I'd just finished a job. I was tired. I was very, very tired.

Even if she was an idol, or a kid, no law in Japan would punish me for blocking her little mouth with everything I had.

"You didn't say anything about three billion yen, right? Right? Ow—Oh, hey, don't run off!"

She'd chomped down on my palm, then swiftly and agilely put some distance between us.

"Wha, wha-wha-wha...?" she stammered. "Where did that come from?! Who—who do you think I am?! I'm the world's *cutest* idol, Yui Saikawa! Do you know who you're dealing with?!"

"Calm down, Saikawa. Yes, my hands are all sticky with your incredibly cute saliva, but I'm not going to swab it and keep it forever or anything. I'm just tired and want you to shut up. That's all."

"Waaaaaaaaugh! I thought you were a detective, but you're a pervert! ...Hah! Wait, are you the criminal who sent me that notice?! Waaaaaugh! You're not just a pervert; you're a thief! Somebody, get me a policeman! Please call the police!"

"Ha-ha. Sorry, but the police and I are already on good terms."

"N-no! Are you saying this country is already corrupt all the way down?! That the police and the lawyers and the politicians are all on the side of the panty stealers?!"

"Hey, whoa, hold on. Now you're combining your 'pervert' and 'thief' accusations into 'panty stealer'? That's a crime that'll get me in trouble with other prisoners after they throw me in jail, so don't try to pin me with a lie! I'm not a pervert or a thief to begin with!"

"Uh, no. You've got two thousand years of hard labor for the crime of wanton perversion." A stone-cold voice calmed me right down.

At that point, I noticed that no one was coming within a set radius of us.

"...Natsunagi, I'm not the bad guy here."

"That's what they all say."

Apparently, my new partner was also a lot harsher than she looked.

◆ A simple job: Protect a three-billion-yen family treasure

"Erm, ahem! I apologize for losing my composure yesterday!"

We really had been tired that day, so Natsunagi and I had come to meet with our client—Yui Saikawa—on another day. She'd invited us to her house, and we'd settled in, facing each other across a table.

And yet...

"Why are you so far away?! This table is a couple of yards long, at least!"

"What, really?! I don't think so!"

"Then why are we shouting?!"

"Because we couldn't hear each other if we talked normally! Obviously!"

"Which suggests that the problem is with your house!"

Long story short, this was Yui Saikawa's house—although it would be better described as a mansion. Maybe even a castle.

After we'd gone through the massive front gate, it was several kilometers before we reached the door of the actual house. Once we were inside, the foyer ceiling was at the top of a wellhole so high it might have breached the stratosphere, and the bathroom she let us use was so spacious that several big adults could have spent the night in there.

That was how magnificent, glorious, and brilliant Yui Saikawa's home was. In other words, she was one of your "rich young heiresses." She must have grown up pampered and doted on, so it made sense that she'd call herself "the cutest." ...Did it, actually?

Well, never mind that. At any rate, the day after Natsunagi and I met her in front of the train station, we'd gone to her house to hear her *request*.

However, before that...

"Did you hurt your left eye?" I asked after we'd reseated ourselves across the table from each other instead of at the ends (should've done that in the first place).

Saikawa's left eye was covered with an eye patch, as it had been the day before as well. Now that I thought about it, I remembered that even when she was on TV or gracing the covers of magazines, she wore a heart-shaped eye patch.

"Oh, this is... Hmm, it's like...part of my public persona? Or something like that." Saikawa smiled wryly. "It's an idol-eat-idol world out there, you know."

If she was keeping that up even out of public view, she must be a real professional.

"Come to think of it, quite a while back, I had to wear an eye patch after an injury, too."

"Well, shelving that topic for now."

"Hey, if anyone's gonna say that, I think it should be me."

...Eh, never mind. Let's just get on with it.

"I apologize for hastily calling out to you," Saikawa said. "You see, there isn't much time left."

"Oh, right, you were talking about a three-billion-yen diamond being stolen?" I replied, remembering what Saikawa had said in front of the station the day before.

"It's a sapphire, not a diamond... Um, were you listening?"

Whoops—she caught me. Frankly, my fatigue had won out yesterday... well, more like I was still mostly in my own head. Either way, I hadn't been very focused on her request.

I was doing my best to stay calm in front of Natsunagi, but I'm only human.

I'd thought my former partner was dead. Then I learned her heart, at least, was alive...and right now, it was beating right next to me.

That fact alone was more than enough to process. Although, if I'd said anything that sentimental, my old partner probably would have laughed at me.

"And you're the assistant, aren't you? My business is with the detective…"

Harsh. But not wrong.

For the past four years, I've never been anything more than the assistant, and even now, the detective is—

"—Heh-heh! That's right. You may entrust all your worries to this ace detective, Nagisa Natsunagi!"

Natsunagi crossed her arms triumphantly, looking smug.

Geez, where is this self-confidence coming from?

"Now then, Miss Saikawa. Would you tell us about the matter in detail?"

That said, if she was into it, there was no need for me to be a wet blanket. I am just the assistant, after all.

"Well, you see…"

Then Saikawa began to tell us what had prompted her to bring her request to us.

"I see."

After we'd heard the whole story, Natsunagi nodded.

According to Saikawa, this was what had happened.

One day, a letter had been delivered to this grand mansion, the Saikawa residence. *"On the day of Yui Saikawa's dome concert, I will relieve you of a sapphire whose market value is three billion yen."*

I didn't know any thieves went out of their way to send calling cards nowadays, but here we were. We'd just have to roll with it.

At any rate, this was a clear advance notice of a crime, and that crime would take place on the day of active idol Yui Saikawa's dome concert (which was scheduled to take place in a week). She wanted us to head it off before it happened.

Still, what had brought her to us, specifically? Was it my talent for getting into trouble, or had that heart summoned her?

"Do you have any idea what that three-billion-yen sapphire might be?"

"Yes. I'm certain it's our family treasure, the Miracle Sapphire. It's in the vault."

Vault, family treasure, Miracle Sapphire. All those words were tailor-made for an incident like this one.

"I have that big concert next Sunday, so no one will be home. I think they plan to use that opportunity to steal the sapphire."

...For someone who'd made careful plans, the criminal seemed to have given them all away in that notice. Seemed counterintuitive.

Or did it mean they were confident they'd be able to pull off the theft even if they sent advance notice? A thrill seeker might go for something like this.

"But if you know when the crime's going to take place, couldn't you just beef up security on that day? This house must have an army of private security."

On the way to this very room, we'd seen brawny-looking men in suits all over the place. If they were already taking care of it, we shouldn't have to come into this at all.

"No, as I said, that's not possible. My concert is on the day of the crime."

"Hmm? Oh, you mean your security personnel are going to be guarding you at the venue?"

"Oh, no. They're huge fans, so seeing me sing and dance is more important to them than protecting a three-billion-yen sapphire."

"Then you should fire them all!"

This was one heck of a request. It was completely unfair.

I stood up.

"Wait, Kimizuka." Unexpectedly, it was Natsunagi who stopped me. "She's been kind enough to come to us. Why don't we hear her out a little longer?"

"...What's going on? You're really taking the reins."

Had just introducing herself as an ace detective made her bolder? Nothing's wrong with being a go-getter, but... She didn't have to get deeply involved in this case. There was no guarantee she wouldn't regret it.

I'd been getting dragged into things for eighteen years, and so I and the formerly invincible ace detective were one thing. On the other hand, Natsunagi was an ordinary person, and this job might end up being too much for her.

Natsunagi put her lips close to my ear and whispered. "I mean, look. Look at her *house*. So if she has a request for us…"

…*Oh. I get you. Well, yeah, the pay would probably be generous, but…*

"This isn't a job you do for money, you know."

"But we do need money, don't we? There's also no telling what jobs we'll get after this."

She had a definite point. After those three years of wandering, I probably understood the importance of money better than anyone.

But did that mean…?

Was Natsunagi prepared for that? For a life like the three years Siesta and I had spent together? She might be forfeiting her chance at a normal future—

"I want a new swimsuit…"

"Hey."

…Well, never mind. Even if our goals were different, money actually was important.

I sat down again—and not because I wanted to see Natsunagi's new swimsuit. No, really, it wasn't.

Besides…

…this was a request from none other than the "idol from Japón," Yui Saikawa.

The tune Siesta had hummed two years ago seemed to stick in my ears.

"Then is that what we're talking about? On the day of the concert, you want Natsunagi and me to be here, guarding your vault?"

"Oh, yes, something like that."

Hey, you wanna give us something to work with? I finally got motivated and everything.

"Actually, wouldn't it be better to leave that to the police?"

"I did speak with them about it, but all I had was the advance notice. They wouldn't pay attention."

…I guess they wouldn't. Ordinarily, the police only take action after something's happened.

On the other hand—and I'll admit this is a very mercenary perspective—there was a lot of money in this situation. If she flashed some of that, I get the feeling she could get them to reconsider.

"Bribing the police. That's certainly an idea I'd expect you to have, Mr. Pervert," said Saikawa.

"I didn't even say anything."

"True, if one has no bread, she could just buy the baker."

"Even Marie Antoinette would keel over at that one!"

Her face was cute, but this girl had zero respect for the entire world.

Smoothly picking her teacup up with her left hand, Saikawa elegantly sipped her tea. Although I hated to admit it, the gesture really suited her.

"And so, I'd like to show you the vault now."

Even as I wondered why she felt the need to say "and so," I knew that thread of conversation was a dead end, so I got up, following Saikawa's lead.

However, well, still…

"Hey, Saikawa." If nothing else, it would be best to get this particular question cleared up right now. "Why is the child the one placing this request?"

We were talking with Yui Saikawa—not her dad, and not her mom.

The Saikawa family treasure was in danger of being stolen, so why were there no adults at this meeting?

It was a completely natural question, and Saikawa explained:

"My parents passed away three years ago. I am the current head of the Saikawa family."

She gave the same smile she wore all the time on TV.

I bet it sucks to be an idol singer, I thought.

◆ I won't die

After that, with Saikawa as our guide, we saw the vault, got a brief tour of the house, exchanged contact information, then adjourned for the day.

On the way back from the Saikawa residence…

"What did you think?" I asked Natsunagi as we walked side by side through the dusk.

"About what?"

"Do you think you'll be able to resolve this request?"

"If I said it wasn't what I thought it would be, would you get mad?" she asked.

"You think I'd be mad?"

I'd told Natsunagi not to try to be anybody's replacement, and she'd still stepped up and taken the role of detective. I'm sure part of it was due to momentum. Part of it was also the heat of the moment.

But this out-of-the-blue request wasn't the type most ordinary detectives would have taken. No wonder she was bewildered.

"I was kidding. Still, detectives have it rough, don't they?"

"Yeah, you may not be able to go back to your life as a normal high schooler."

"I thought detectives only, you know...searched for runaway pet cats and that sort of thing."

"I think you owe every detective in the country an apology." That said, she wasn't entirely wrong.

"Yesterday..." Natsunagi stopped under a streetlight. "I had a dream—about Siesta. It was probably because of everything that just happened." She glanced at me.

"...I see. How was she doing?"

"She was incredibly beautiful, for one thing. I was kinda blown away."

"I know, right?"

"Uh, I don't get why *you're* bragging about that, Kimizuka."

By the way, Natsunagi had never met Siesta, so she probably heard what I was saying the previous day, formed a mental image of her, and dreamed about that version.

"Did you two talk about anything?"

"Um, actually, we fought like crazy..."

"When you meet someone in a dream, you're not supposed to come out swinging, y'know."

Although, I'm pretty sure I get it.

After all, Siesta and Natsunagi seem like complete opposites: a logical type and an emotional type, I guess you'd call it. You could say they share a lack of common sense, but anyway.

"We had a vicious, no-holds-barred argument. Neither of us would back down, and things got...a little physical."

"Glad I didn't have to see that."

"But in the end…"

I heard Natsunagi inhale.

"…she told me to take care of you."

From under the streetlight, a steady gaze was focused on me.

"…So, what, I caused that fight?"

Vaguely embarrassed, I tried to say something random and stupid to move the conversation along, but then…

"…! N-no, nuh-uh. We weren't fighting over you or anything, Kimizuka."

"Huh? What's with that reaction? Now I'm even more worried…"

"Aaaaaah, aaaaaaah! We are done talking about this!"

—And with that, the topic was folded up and put away. Natsunagi fanned her face with her hands, although it was pretty cool at this hour. "Anyway! Let's do this thing together. Me as the detective, and you as my assistant."

"Yeah, yeah. You do have that swimsuit riding on this."

"You want to see me wearing it, don't you, Kimizuka?"

"Yep. There is nothing I want more than to see you in a swimsuit."

"Ugh, you could at least try to sound convincing." Natsunagi's cold eyes peered into my face. "But I guess it's all right."

"It is?"

"Yeah. If we manage to complete this request, wanna go to the beach together?"

"Don't jinx us. You'll get yourself killed talking like that."

"No, I won't."

Natsunagi trotted a few steps ahead, then turned back to face me.

"I won't die. Whatever happens, I won't die and leave you behind."

Natsunagi set her hand over the left side of her chest. "Cross my heart."

"Okay."

A crescent moon was floating in the pitch-black sky ahead of us, far and distant as we walked forward.

◆ The gossip doesn't stop

The next day, I went to a CD store in the big local shopping mall on my own.

I was there for Yui Saikawa's albums and DVDs of her concerts. A lot of the time, gathering information on clients turns out to be a necessary part of completing a job. Natsunagi could have come with me today, too, but… Well, these dull jobs belong to the assistant. At least they did for those three years.

"She has quite a discography."

Just inside the shop's entrance, they'd set up a display featuring Saikawa. All the CDs she'd released over the past few years were lined up there, and a monitor was showing her singing and dancing at one of her concerts.

"I'm impressed she can dance with that eye patch on."

What had she called it…part of her "*public persona*"? There was a heart-shaped patch covering Saikawa's left eye, but from the way she was bounding around the stage, it didn't seem to affect her at all.

"—Kimizuka."

"……!"

Suddenly, someone spoke to me from behind, right next to my ear, and I flinched.

"I see, I see. Kimizuka likes it when someone blows in his hear. Duly noted."

"Don't randomly make things up to randomly convince yourself—Saikawa."

When I turned around, the girl who was currently showing on the monitor was standing there, looking smug for some reason.

"You sure you should be here without a disguise? You'll set off a stampede."

"I have my hood up. It's fine. You wouldn't think it, but people don't notice," Saikawa said proudly. "So what brings you here, Kimizuka? Can't stop thinking about me? Have you become a fan? Ooh, have you fallen for me? I'm sorry, but romance is off-limits for idols; please try again in the next world, okay?"

"Don't dump me when I haven't even confessed. I'm just here to do field research."

Apparently, the self-proclaimed cutest idol didn't have a trace of doubt regarding her own cuteness.

"Field research, hmm? I see, yes. You're just like me, then."

"You too, Saikawa?"

"Yes, as a matter of fact, my latest single just came out last week. I was curious about how it was selling."

What a pro. She might have nothing but contempt for the world, but she seemed serious about her job as an idol, at least.

…But why would she physically come to the store to do field research in this day and age? I mean, what I was doing wasn't much different, so I couldn't really talk, but still.

"You aren't with the detective today."

"Nope. There's no rule that says detectives and assistants have to be together all the time."

"Is that right?" Saikawa said, coming up to stand on my right. "She really is gorgeous, isn't she?"

"Well, on the outside, yeah. The jury's still out on the rest."

"Oh, Natsunagi is as well, but I was referring to myself."

"You've got no qualms about blowing your own horn, huh?"

Her confidence was so high it was actually refreshing. In fact, maybe any idol worth her salt should be a little like this.

"Of course not. A girl needs at least this much faith in herself to survive the idol industry." Saikawa gave a world-weary shrug, turning both palms up. "Rivals slash up your costumes and hide tacks in your shoes on a daily basis."

"I don't need to know all the backstage drama, thanks."

"And then, from what I'm told, those rivals will all vanish from public life by the next day."

"That's a coincidence, right? It's gotta be."

"Are you in favor of gun regulation in Japan, Kimizuka? Or against it?"

"Don't bring that debate into this particular discussion, all right?! You're freaking me out! And it doesn't matter whether I'm in favor or not; owning guns isn't legal in Japan anyway."

...He says, turning a blind eye to his past.

"Heh-heh. I like you, Kimizuka; your reactions are funny. I was joking. It was only a joke." Saikawa looked up at me with an affectionate smile.

"I couldn't quite tell where the joke started and ended."

"The joke was the part where I said I like you."

"Okay, okay. I know contempt when I see it."

"Ah-ha-ha. What I said just now was the actual joke." Laughing, Saikawa reached out toward the display in front of us.

As always, this middle school kid was hard to pin down, and it wasn't easy to tell what she really meant and what was just her public face. Watching Saikawa cheerfully test-listen to her own CD out of the corner of my eye, I thought that being an idol really was a tough job.

"Probably should've asked before," I said, "but are you okay? With everything?"

"Pardon? Is what okay?"

"You've got that big concert on Sunday. And now you get a notice from a thief, and, you know... Mentally, how are you doing?"

Saikawa's parents were gone. This situation was so heavy for a girl who was still in middle school to carry on her own.

"...I'm all right." Still facing forward, Saikawa softly put a hand to her left eye. "I'm not alone, you see."

"......?"

"Mama and Papa are always—" She was letting me catch a glimpse of that slightly unusual side of herself, but not for long. "You're kind, aren't you, Kimizuka?" Spinning to face me, Saikawa peeked up into my face.

"Kind? That's not one I get very often."

"It's possible a human heart has begun to grow in you."

"What am I, a robot? Just now learning these mysterious *emotions* after living with the professor?"

"This is called 'joy.' That's called 'sorrow.' Those tears are your 'heart.'"

"And now we're in a tearjerker sci-fi movie."

"And after all of it, you were built merely to sacrifice yourself to destroy our enemies."

"Ouch, that was really unfair... Give me back my emotional character development."

I poked her head lightly, and Saikawa giggled. "You really are funny, Kimizuka," she said, tucking her hair behind her ears, inside her hood. The way she intentionally used her opposite hand for the gesture, crossing herself, boosted her flirtatiousness by 20 percent.

"I'm not falling for a cheap trick like that."

"Heh-heh. I wonder if you'll still be able to say that after you've *watched DVDs bursting with my charms.*"

"They're just concert DVDs; don't make it weird."

Although, once she'd said that, I felt hesitant about buying them in front of her. I turned on my heel, planning to go somewhere else and try again later.

"Well, I'm off."

"All right. See you later. And thank you for taking my request," she said behind me. Still facing away from her, I raised a hand in response.

After I left the store, I got out my phone and tapped my contacts list.

"...This may be trickier than I thought."

Finally, after one, two, three rings, she picked up.

"Hello?"

"Uh, do you have a minute—Ms. Fuubi?"

◆ That's "Yui-nya Quality"

A few days later, it was Saturday, and Natsunagi and I had gone to the dome that was serving as the venue. Yui Saikawa's concert was the following day.

"Hurry up. The rehearsal's gonna start."

As we climbed the long stairway to the dome, I called back to Natsunagi, who was slumped wearily a dozen or so steps below me.

"When you said you'd come without so much as a towel or a glow stick, I thought it was bad, but I can't believe you aren't even trying to make it to the rehearsal before it starts... And you call yourself a fan?"

"Uh, no. I don't." Natsunagi heaved a big sigh. She was glaring at me for some reason. "Come on, don't you think you're mixing business with pleasure?"

"What do you mean?"

"That!" Finally climbing the stairs, Natsunagi pointed sharply at my clothes. "What is this? Why are you wearing a Saikawa concert T-shirt? Why do you have several towels with venue-specific designs around your neck? What is that mass of penlights you've got tied around your waist? What about the wristbands? The hat? The sneakers?"

Apparently, she had quite a few complaints building up, and they all came out in a rush.

"They're all Yui-nya concert merch."

"'Yui-nya'?!"

All her fans called her that, to show their affection.

"Okay, what exactly did you do this past week? You didn't come to school, and you didn't respond when I tried to get ahold of you. When you finally did reply, you just said we were going to see the rehearsal the day before the show..."

"Uh, well, I was watching all the past episodes of TV programs Yui-nya had been in, and the next thing I knew, it was today—"

"Okay, I'm double-killing you."

"Ghk, stop... Strangling me with my towels is—against the rules... gweeeh..."

I smacked Natsunagi's shoulder in surrender.

"Do you know what's happening tomorrow?" Natsunagi looked up at me crankily from one step below me on the stairs.

"Well, it's Yui-nya's concert, right?"

"—. That too, but... That isn't why we're here, remember? The crime is supposed to take place then. We have to protect the Miracle Sapphire from the criminal. Am I wrong?"

I see. Natsunagi was probably trying to say we were in the wrong place, since this was the day before the theft.

"I get what you're saying, Natsunagi, but some truths only become apparent by learning the background of the client, right?"

"Well..." She didn't seem completely convinced yet. "Would you usually go this far, though? Begging Saikawa to let us watch a rehearsal...?"

"Once you take a job, give it everything you have. Besides, we'll have to guard Yui-nya's house on the day of the concert. Let's enjoy the heck out of today to make up for it."

"Um, you said 'enjoy'..."

I didn't need all that "business or pleasure" and "separation of church and state" right now.

"You were weirding her out; I know it."

"I didn't weird her out. She was flustered, but..."

"Uh, that means the same thing."

Really? Well, I still think we're fine.

Even a week ago, depending on how you looked at it, we'd been close enough to have a fun conversation... Depending on how you looked at it.

"You can bet the opening number's going to be 'Raspberry × Grizzly.'"

"Look, I don't know her standard setlist."

All right. The rehearsal was about to start.

Tugging the perplexed Natsunagi by the hand, I hurried into the venue.

"The Love Express just won't stooop! ♪"

"Woo-woooooo!"

"Wait for me at the end of the line, okay? ♪"

"Puff, puff!"

"Speeding past the local trains! ♪"

"Don't leave meee!"

"No stalling allowed! ♪ On the Nine-Star! ♪"

"Yeah!!!!!!!"

From a spot near the back of the stands, I waved a pink glow stick at the stage wildly.

As enthusiastic as she was, you'd never think it was a rehearsal. I was putting more energy into my cheering, too. From the next seat over, Natsunagi was judging the hell out of me, but I couldn't let that get me down.

"Thank you very much! That was 'The Nine-Star Stops in November!' from my second album!"

"Wait, why's it's stopping?" Next to me, Natsunagi muttered, straight-faced, "Didn't she just say the Love Express won't stop?"

"Details, details. This is Yui-nya Quality."

"Yui-nya Quality."

I'd taken a full course in her songs over the past week, and most of them were like this.

Catchy melodies and off-the-wall lyrics. The more you chewed them over, the more they numbed your taste buds while giving you the illusion of flavor—that was Yui-nya Quality.

"You too, Pervert! Thank you!" Yui-nya waved enthusiastically from the stage toward the seats.

"Hey, Natsunagi, she talked to you!"

"She's one thousand percent talking about you!"

"Nah, you just couldn't hide your vibes from her."

"……! Hey, I'm not the one being weird here!" Natsunagi's face was bright red, and she tried to kick me with her high heel.

"Hey, why'd you wear heels to a concert? It's gonna be hard to jump around in those."

"I'm not jumping around! Your head is what's jumping around!"

Rude. I just wanted to enjoy the concert.

"All right, and now for the next song!" Just then, Yui-nya signaled the sound crew with a glance.

"Here it comes."

"What now?"

"Hey, come on, Natsunagi, we just heard 'Eighty-One.' That means the next song is…?"

"I told you, I don't know her setlist. And abbreviating 'The Nine-Star Stops in November!' as 'Eighty-One' is the geekiest thing I've ever heard. Nine times 'Novem' equals eighty-one? Come on."

Just what I'd expect from an ace detective—she understood instantly.

"So next up is Yui-nya's special song. We came here today so we could hear this, remember?"

"That's news to me."

I see; I guess I hadn't told Natsunagi yet.

Actually, well…I hadn't been planning to mention it in the first place.

Not to Natsunagi nor to anybody else. This way made things easier, now that I was a pitiful fanboy who'd accidentally gotten hooked on *Yui-nya* in the course of doing his job.

Or at least, I was *pretending* to be…

"Don't you know? During this song, for just the last chorus, Yui-nya removes her seal."

"Seal?"

Yes. The seal Yui-nya—or rather, Yui Saikawa—placed on herself. Her secret.

"Now then, please listen—to 'Sapphire ★ Phantasm.'"

An up-tempo intro played, and Saikawa began running through light-footed dance steps.

"Like a mirror reflecting the blue Eaaarth… ♪"

For the past week, I'd listened to Saikawa's songs constantly and, more importantly, pored over all the videos in which she appeared.

As I did so, I'd discovered just one thing—one big thing—that felt off.

I'd sensed something was wrong the day I first met her, and it had only grown from there.

Yui Saikawa is lying.

I was here today to make sure.

Before long, the A section ended, and the song reached the bridge. Just then—

"Huh? Kimizuka… Look."

Next to me, Natsunagi leaned forward slightly.

A man was standing on the left side of the stage, back in the wings. He was wearing sunglasses and dressed all in black. He didn't look like a member of staff.

"Isn't that man kind of weird?"

That's a detective for you; she's got good instincts. However…

"Hmm? What's up?"

…I pretended not to notice.

Sorry, Natsunagi. Wait just a little longer.

Then the B section ended, and just as the C section was beginning…the man in black started walking toward Saikawa. And then—

"Huh?! ...Eeeeeeeeeeeeeeeeek!" Saikawa's scream echoed across the whole hall, amplified by her mic.

"Hey, who's that?! Get him!"

Just in the nick of time, right before the man reached Saikawa, the security staff grabbed him.

"...That's what I thought." I'd been feeling that dissonance all week. Now that I'd seen this in person, I was sure. I was glad I'd come here today, even if I'd had to bull my way through.

"Kimizuka! Hurry!" Natsunagi shouted.

Saikawa was crouched down and looking dazed, while Natsunagi kicked off her heels and dashed to the stage, barefoot.

It was a beautiful, and very human, reaction.

Nevertheless, a detective has no use for those passionate feelings. Kindness and consideration can sometimes come back to bite you—although she didn't know that yet.

"Are you okay?" I asked the frightened Saikawa, following Natsunagi up onto the stage.

"Oh, Mr. Pervert... Thank you."

"Don't keep calling me a pervert after what just happened."

If she could crack jokes, though, that was a good sign. I didn't want this to end up traumatizing her.

"Still, you never know what might happen. Guarding the vault tomorrow is important, but I'd ramp up security here, too. Show us around backstage later."

"All right..." Saikawa didn't seem to have fully recovered from the shock yet. She nodded weakly.

I did feel bad, but the things detectives do are always guided by logic. *I want to make sure you understand that.*

...Even if I am just the assistant.

◆ Sunday showdown

The next morning was Sunday—the day the Miracle Sapphire, the Saikawa family treasure, was scheduled to be stolen.

At the request of Yui Saikawa, Natsunagi and I had agreed to guard her house.

Right now, we were in a taxi, headed toward *our destination*.

"Kimizuka... Is what you told me yesterday really true?" Natsunagi was sitting beside me in the back seat.

The previous day, after the rehearsal was over, she and I had gone to the same café we'd visited before and discussed our game plan for today. While we did that, I'd also shared with Natsunagi the *secret* Yui Saikawa was hiding.

"Aren't you here because you believed me?"

"Technically, yes. But is *the other place* going to be all right? We can't just leave it empty..."

"Yeah, I've got that covered, too. It sounds like Ms. Fuubi is going over there."

"I've been meaning to ask you: Who exactly is she?"

"She's an army of one."

"That sounds like an explanation, but it's really not."

Sorry, but it's not like I know everything about her, either. Just that she's someone you can count on.

"Is something worrying you?" I asked.

"Nothing really. I'm just kinda...not completely satisfied with this."

"With what?"

"Ultimately, Kimizuka, you're trying to resolve this incident. But I'm the detective." As she spoke, Natsunagi gazed out the window at the sun, which was just above the horizon.

"That's just how it happened this time."

"Was it really?"

"Yeah. I'm sure the day when you're the one who saves me will come along pretty soon."

If I had to say, I've always been in that position until now. If I don't work a little every once in a while, that heart of yours is going to get mad at me.

"It's almost time for the show."

I glanced at my watch. Talking Ms. Fuubi and her crew around, and enlisting the help of a certain other individual, had taken up more time than I'd expected.

"If we don't make it there in time, this'll go south real quick…"

The first number of Yui Saikawa's concert would be starting soon.

"So you actually do care about it?" Natsunagi seemed to be satisfied regarding the previous subject; the corners of her mouth quirked up a little.

"Only for the job. I don't care about 'Raspberry × Grizzly.' I told you back at the café, remember?"

"You did, but seriously, could you really do all that as an act? You really creeped me out yesterday, Kimizuka."

"Don't say it that way. Nothing hurts more than having a high school girl call you creepy."

"I was just thinking maybe we were actually headed over there because of your hobby again."

"Hey, that's not fair. If it wasn't for a job, I wouldn't go near the *dome*."

As we traded verbal jabs, we were racing toward our destination: *Yui Saikawa's dome concert*.

We already had measures in place, but it would be pointless if we didn't get there in time.

"Hey, could you make it fast?" I told the taxi driver.

"…Fasten your seatbelts."

The hair under his cap was blond, and I could see his cloudy eyes glance at us in the rearview mirror.

"I hope we make it in time for 'Eighty-One,'" I said.

"You sure you're not just into her?"

◆ Sapphire ☆ Phantasm

"…This is nothing like the rehearsal."

When we reached the dome and opened the doors to the hall, over-whelming light and sound swept over us. Rainbow-colored spotlights scattered reflections everywhere, and the vibrations thudded heavily in the pit of my stomach.

This was a different world, a circular hole cut out of the ordinary.

The ruler of that world was the idol singer—Yui Saikawa.

She was dressed in a frilly costume, and hundreds of shining glow sticks were being offered up to her. If I remembered right, the number she was singing in her irresistible voice was her latest single.

We were coming up on the second half of the concert, so she was probably about to drop a hit medley on them.

"Hey!"

A tug on my sleeve brought my mind back to reality.

"Where are our seats?!" Natsunagi was standing on tiptoe to yell into my ear. We couldn't hear otherwise.

"You know we don't have any! We don't even have tickets!"

"Oh..."

Then how had we managed to infiltrate this hall? We'd had the security staff *go to sleep* for a little while.

"You think those people are all right?!"

"They're fine! *He* doesn't want to do stuff like that anymore, and he wouldn't get anything out of it!"

Apparently, he'd struck a bargain with Ms. Fuubi regarding his future, among other things.

Just then, the number ended, and after the applause, silence fell for a moment. This was our chance.

"Natsunagi, let's go." Reverting to a whisper, I thumped Natsunagi on the shoulder.

"Huh? Go where?"

"We'll get as close to the stage as we can."

The previous day, thanks to my excuse of watching the rehearsal, I'd casually done a preliminary inspection of the arena.

We crouched down and started moving as quickly as we could without drawing attention.

"Hey, isn't that bag in the way? You could have left it in the car." Natsunagi pointed at my clutch bag.

"Oh, well, not really."

"So what's in there?"

"Something I don't want to use." Or to be more precise, something I hoped we wouldn't be forced to use.

"Huh. Well, it doesn't really matter what it is... And? That one song's still a ways away, isn't it?"

"Yeah, since it comes after 'Eighty-One.'"

"Come to think of it, you're right... So you actually were working at that rehearsal yesterday."

"You're too suspicious. Well, that's not a bad thing for a detective."

"Yes. Maybe so."

The new song began.

At the rehearsal, "Eighty-One" had been after this; if anything was going to happen, it would be during the number after that, "Sapphire ★ Phantasm." We had about ten minutes left.

We walked on quietly, being careful not to attract suspicion.

"What's the point of getting close to the stage, though?" Natsunagi asked, right by my ear.

"Frankly, we're gonna have to wing it. I don't know what's about to happen. Maybe nothing, and all our worries will be pointless. That means we'll just have to do our best with what we've got."

All we could do was keep our eyes peeled for that moment—that was it. To that end, we'd lurk as near Saikawa as possible right now.

Just a little closer than *they* were, even if we didn't even know where that was.

"Thank you so much, all of you!"

A cheer went up. The number was over.

Next up was finally "Eighty-One"... *Maybe we should pick up the pace.*

"Now that everyone's all fired up, I think it's about time we brought out the song you've been waiting for!"

Saikawa gave a brief comment from the stage, and then the song that began to play was—

"Without further ado—'Sapphire ★ Phantasm'!"

What?!

This wasn't the order we'd heard at the rehearsal... Dammit. We'd used up too much time earlier.

"N-no!"

"Yeah, this is bad. Let's hurry, Natsunagi."

"You were looking forward to 'Eighty-One' so much!"

"I wasn't looking forward to it!"

This was no time for joking around. Of course Natsunagi knew that, too, as we headed toward the stage.

"Like a mirror reflecting the blue Eaaarth... ♪"

The voltage in the venue spiked, the enthusiasm fueled by an explosion of noise and light.

"Sapphire ★ Phantasm" was idol singer Yui Saikawa's biggest hit and her specialty. During this song, *she always did something very special onstage.*

That was bound to be the *trigger.*

Natsunagi and I had come here to stop it.

"If the *group* you talked about are hiding, where would they be?"

"No idea. They might be in the audience, or they could be hiding in the wings, like that man was yesterday."

The previous day, I'd had Saikawa and the staff show us the backstage area and various facilities, but it had only given us more options. The two of us weren't enough to cover all those possibilities on our own.

That said, we couldn't afford to take too much time on our end. After all, this was happening right on the heels of the day before, and *they* had to be incredibly busy *on their end* as well. We'd just have to make do with our limited personnel and limited time.

"I hid it in my secret treasure chest... ♪"

She'd reached the C section already. It wouldn't be long until the last chorus, the time when her *seal* was released. If anything was going to happen, it would be soon.

"Okay, we're here."

We'd finally reached the stage-side aisle, beyond the arena seats.

Where? Where were they?

Straining my eyes, I searched for someone who might not even be there. But the rainbow spotlights made it hard to see, and the blaring music from the nearby speakers chipped away at my concentration.

"......!" Natsunagi was saying something, but the place was so loud I couldn't hear her at all.

Dammit, this is even worse than I thought.

They were probably around here, somewhere close. But there wasn't much time left.

I'd underestimated the challenges. I'd thought that if I strained my eyes and ears once I was there, I'd probably find them, but I'd put too much faith in my experience. *So your brain shuts down this bad when your sight and hearing aren't working properly?*

It was no good: The sound and the light were starting to give me a roaring headache. I was even getting nauseous.

I wanted to enlist Natsunagi's help, but thanks to the music, I wouldn't even be able to communicate accurately.

I needed a plan, some kind of plan...

No, wait.

Of course. Even in a situation like this, there might be one person—

"It's me! Can you hear me?!"

Holding my temples, I yelled at *him*, the one we'd hired as our chauffeur. He couldn't see, but he'd said as long as he could hear, he could drive. Right now, after putting the security guards to sleep, he was probably having a smoke somewhere near the arena.

Of course, he was several hundred meters away from us...but to him, a distance like that was nothing.

Even in the midst of this ear-splitting noise, my voice was bound to reach him. In fact, he'd even be able to hear the heartbeat of our hidden enemy.

"—Bat! Where's the enemy?!" My pocket vibrated.

The notification from my messaging app was just a single "→."

An arrow? Some sort of code?

...Oh! I got it!

Sprinting away from the startled Natsunagi, I ran up onto the stage, where Saikawa was.

During the final chorus, she *removed the patch over her left eye.*

It was her biggest performance of the day, a special number where she gave her all.

A cheer went up.

This was Yui Saikawa's seal. The secret she'd hidden from us.

"—*The Miracle Sapphire with a market value of three billion yen is Yui Saikawa's left eye!*"

As I spoke, I pulled Saikawa to me, evading *an incoming crossbow bolt.*

◆ Thus spoke the super-idol

So. About this incident.

Where should I start; what should I explain first to give you the most accurate picture? Whose perspective should I tell it from, if I'm going to make it easy to understand?

Unfortunately, I'm just an assistant, a student at most. Definitely not a novelist. Even if I was giving a full account of this incident to somebody, I'm sure I'd be a terrible storyteller.

There are just too many lies, secrets, and deceptions—too much information hovering in the ether around this case. I'm sure the plot would make no sense.

"No, that's all my fault." After the concert, Saikawa had called Natsunagi and me to her dressing room. Kneeling formally in front of us, she looked down apologetically. "I should have told you everything from the beginning instead of going off on my own. That's why things turned out this way. I'm afraid I've caused you both a lot of trouble. I'm sorry."

With that, Saikawa bowed her head deeply.

"…Um. I still don't completely understand this… Could you explain it?"

Natsunagi raised a hand hesitantly. She must have been embarrassed by the fact that she didn't know the truth of the matter, even though she was a detective.

But I was in the same boat.

My ideas about the truth of this incident, about how we'd ended up here, were still only theory. I'd been waiting this whole time for her to tell us herself.

"Yes, you're right. I should. This may end up being rather long, but please bear with me anyway."

Once again, Saikawa removed her eye patch.

That blue left eye, which reflected everything in the world, was as beautiful as a sapphire.

"Now then, where should I begin my story? Er, yes, I suppose I should start at the beginning, shouldn't I? All right, I'll start with my left eye... Actually, that may end up being the beginning. I received this artificial blue eye as a birthday present from my parents, the year I turned eight...

"...Yes, that's right, Miss Detective. Although I believe you may have noticed it yourself, Mr. Assistant. This is a false eye, not heterochromia. I was born blind in my left eye. As a young child, I had a complex about it that made me very quiet and shy. I was my parents' only daughter, and they got worried about me. They wanted me to have more hope in life, so they gave me an artificial eye the color of sapphire. Bluer than the sea.

"Back then, I was entranced by how beautiful it was. Of course, I didn't let anyone see it in public. Still, simply having this eye gave me confidence in myself, somehow. That was when I began my career as an idol. Mama and Papa were delighted to see that I'd cheered up, and that made me happy, so I put more and more effort into my lessons. *Ah, I finally know what it means to be alive...,* I thought. You may laugh and say I'm exaggerating, but it's true.

"I'm sorry; I've gotten a little off track.

"Long story short, my life as an idol was going smoothly, but that life didn't last long. Three years ago, when I was eleven, my parents died in an accident. They left me a large house, a vast fortune I had no use for, and... my left eye.

"After that, my blue eye was more precious than anything to me. I wanted to keep it carefully hidden inside. That's why I always wear an eye patch... But in my big shows, I decided I would reveal my left eye, just for a moment. If I didn't, and my parents came from heaven to see one of my concerts, I felt like they might not realize it was me.

"This beautiful blue jewel in my eye was the bond that connected me to my parents; I couldn't just go around showing it to other people. That's why I didn't tell you about it.

"I never dreamed that the criminal considered my eye a 'miracle sapphire.' It just so happens that there is a sapphire worth three billion yen in the Saikawa family vault, so I assumed that was what they meant.

"When I think of all the trouble I would have saved you if I'd told you the whole story... I'm truly sorry. And thank you. Thank you so much.

"I was sure the two of you had gone to my house today, so I was a little surprised. I should have known better. You figured out my secret, picked up on the criminal's true objective, and came running. You even pretended it was part of the stage show and kept from scaring the audience.

"I'm so glad I brought my request to you.

"Really and truly—

"—thank you so much."

Once she had come to the end of her story, Saikawa bowed so low that her forehead practically touched the floor.

And there you have it. As she'd said, the "sapphire worth three billion yen" in the advance notice had been not the family treasure, the jewel at the Saikawa residence, but Saikawa's own artificial eye.

The criminal had waited until Saikawa uncovered her shining-blue secret onstage, then attempted to snipe it from a distance.

But as it turned out, the case—the story—had reached its end without any casualties, and the sapphire hadn't been stolen, either. It was an undeniably happy ending.

"It's all right, so…get up, okay?" Natsunagi said.

Saikawa slowly raised her head. Her expression held a mixture of gratitude and apology…and relief, as if she'd finally shaken off a heavy, tenacious burden.

Now we'd settle the matter peacefully, and after exchanging a few words, we'd get a little reward—and then Natsunagi would buy her new swimsuit, and we'd make that trip to the beach. Yes, this case had been safely closed.

There had been some trouble and a few unexpected developments that had caught us off guard and worn us out a bit, but that was hardly anything. During those three years I'd spent with Siesta, my life had been far more risky and violent.

All right—it was time to head back to our peaceful routine. First, Natsunagi and I should probably discuss which beach to go to. That meant we'd be meeting at our usual café.

Just like that...

Now, I could probably have put that whole incident behind me as if nothing had happened. As if I hadn't noticed.

A week ago, before I met Natsunagi and that heart, I'm sure I would have left the dressing room, pretending I knew nothing. That would have been easier, after all. If I did that, my peaceful routine would have been waiting for me.

Unfortunately, though, I was through with ignoring the truth.

Yes, Saikawa had revealed the secret she'd been hiding. But she hadn't yet confessed her lie.

"Listen, Saikawa."

When I said her name, her face turned toward me.

"Yes?"

She tilted her head slightly, gazing at me blankly, innocently.

She was an idol; she could put on any expression with perfect ease. She could smile or cry on demand.

"Is the penalty going to give you any trouble? After all, Natsunagi and I are still alive."

In that instant, all color vanished from Yui Saikawa's face.

◆ What that eye sees

"Wow, geez! Where did that come from, Mr. Assistant?"

Saikawa's face was blank for only a moment before her usual idol smile returned.

She was a real pro; even I was a little scared.

"Are you saying I was trying to kill you two? Ah-ha-ha! I think 'mystery writer' would be a more suitable profession for you, Mr. Assistant." Saikawa smiled. "Oooh, I've always wanted to say that."

"Um, Kimizuka? Saikawa already confessed her secret to us, remember? You didn't tell me any more than that." Of the three of us, Natsunagi was the one who seemed the most bewildered. "You said the criminal was after Saikawa's left eye, not the sapphire. That's why we went to the dome instead of guarding the vault. That's all I heard…"

Right: I hadn't told Natsunagi the whole truth yet, either.

I'd been hoping Saikawa would tell us about it herself, but apparently that was not to be.

"As Natsunagi says, you did tell us about your secret, Saikawa… But you haven't confessed your lie."

"My lie? What do you mean?" Saikawa was listening to me carefully, still wearing that smile.

"Yui Saikawa—*you were working with the criminals from the beginning to kill Natsunagi and me.* Isn't that right?"

"Huh?!" Natsunagi froze up.

"Well, Natsunagi was an incidental target. The enemy was probably after me."

"But…! Do you have any proof?" Detective Natsunagi was talking like the suspect, while Saikawa was as outwardly calm as ever.

Trrrrrrrrrrrrrr—

Just then, the phone in my pocket rang.

"Hello? Kimizuka speaking… Yeah, mm-hmm… Is that right? No, my apologies for the trouble… Thank you. All right, good-bye."

Good. Things had gone well on that end, too.

"Kimizuka, who was that?"

"Oh, Ms. Fuubi. She said they'd just finished removing all *the explosives rigged up in the vault* at the Saikawa residence."

Ms. Fuubi's bomb disposal squad really knew their stuff. They'd gotten through the job without any trouble.

"…! B-but the criminals were after Saikawa's left eye, weren't they? Why would they do that to her house?"

"Like I said, they were after two things. One was Saikawa's sapphire left eye, as I told you. The other…was the lives of the pair who were expected to guard the Saikawa residence. That would be us."

"What does that mean? The criminals weren't planning to go after the sapphire in the vault, but after us, while we were in there?"

"That's it."

They'd probably planned to kill us with a time bomb when we waltzed in there all wide-eyed and clueless. As with that crossbow earlier, the enemy wasn't planning to show themselves directly.

"Basically, that was the lie Saikawa told us. She knew about the criminals' plan all along… Specifically, they gave her the details, and she was supposed to lure us into that vault."

"But, no… What about the proof?" Natsunagi pressed me, as if she didn't want to believe it.

"Ms. Fuubi said she didn't know."

"Huh?"

"She said no one had reported any calling cards sent to the Saikawa residence."

"No… Didn't she say she'd gone to the police, but they wouldn't help? And that was why she'd gone to detectives like us…" Natsunagi looked at Saikawa.

That blue eye didn't waver at all.

That was one of the things that had nagged at me the day I'd first met Saikawa.

She had all that money. For better or worse, any police force that didn't act when she flashed that at them was no police force at all.

After that, when I'd checked with Ms. Fuubi just to make sure, my hunch had been right on target. The police had no idea that a notice had been sent to the Saikawa residence.

Meaning that right from the start, Saikawa had gone *specifically to Natsunagi and me*, instead of to the police. Which, in turn, meant she'd wanted something to do with us, specifically.

True, at that point in time, I still couldn't have said for sure that what she wanted was *our lives*. On the other hand, Natsunagi notwithstanding, there was a reason for people to go after my life. I also had an idea as to who the criminals—our enemies—might be.

"But that can't be right. Saikawa is an idol singer; why would she...? Don't tell me—"

Well, I wouldn't tell her Saikawa was a member of SPES, if that's what she was thinking.

"They probably threatened her."

For the first time, Saikawa's petite shoulders trembled slightly.

"They said, 'If you don't want to lose that left eye, get rid of Kimihiko Kimizuka.'"

That was the condition they'd set. Saikawa's left eye was more important to her than her own life, and she had sold us to the enemy for it.

"Listen, Saikawa. They aren't that soft. They tried to take both."

Specifically, they might have been trying to *destroy* it, rather than steal it. That's why they had shot at it with a crossbow. And their goal in doing so was—

"But why?" Natsunagi broke in. "The criminals—the organization you were talking about, Kimizuka—why would they go after Saikawa's artificial eye? It's pretty, but why would they go that far?"

"Because it's way more than an artificial eye."

"Huh?"

There had to be a reason it was big enough to be a target.

"Isn't that right, Saikawa?" I said. "Tell me, right now, *what can you see?*"

For just a moment, Saikawa glanced at the clutch bag by my feet.

"Is that for self-defense?" When she finally spoke, her voice was as gentle and sweet as ever.

So I was right, huh?

That's an idol for you. *She'd known what I had in my bag*, and even then, she was managing to keep that smile on her face.

"Self-defense?" I replied. "Yeah. See, I've been running into life-threatening situations for ages."

Swiftly shoving a hand into the bag, I used my other hand to push Natsunagi behind me.

I withdrew the handgun and aimed it straight ahead of me—

"I won't give you people my left eye."

—at Yui Saikawa, who was pointing a gun of her own at us.

◆ More than any idol

Saikawa's gun was aimed right between my eyes.

"I see. *So that's how they threatened you*, huh?"

As far as Saikawa was concerned, Natsunagi and I were the enemies—the very people who were trying to steal her sapphire left eye, or so they'd led her to believe. Then they'd offered to help her dispose of us, and she'd accepted.

"Geez, they even gave you a gun?"

"No, I bought it myself."

"Idols shouldn't have their own handguns."

"What, isn't it a normal girlish hobby?"

"I can tell you categorically that it's not."

…No, this was no time for a bantering contest.

"Saikawa, we're not the enemy. I know you know this. Did you forget we protected you a minute ago?"

"That was… I mean, I'm sure you were only trying to make me lower my guard…"

"There was no need for that. If I hadn't run in right then, that crossbow bolt would have nailed your left eye. If I was really your enemy, would I go out of my way to make extra work for myself?"

"That's… That's…"

"Listen, Saikawa. Even if you kill us, it won't do you any good. After we're dead, *the real enemy* is going to take your left eye."

"That's not true!" Saikawa screamed, releasing her gun's safety with her thumb. "It isn't true. Otherwise— Otherwise, I…"

Her expression was resolute, but there was just a slight tremble in her voice.

"Saikawa, you know that left eye isn't just a prosthetic, don't you?"

Saikawa bit her lip. She didn't answer my question.

"What do you mean?" Behind me, I heard Natsunagi's quivering voice.

"It means SPES has a good reason to go after it."

"You said something like that earlier, but… You mean…"

"Right. In simple terms, Saikawa's eye is like *that guy's ear*."

"Him? ...! So that's what this is..." Natsunagi seemed to have reached the same conclusion I had, and words deserted her.

"That left eye... That pseudoeye *can see through physical objects.* Isn't that right, Saikawa?"

That was why they were obsessed with it.

I had no idea how Saikawa's parents had gotten ahold of it...but however it happened, SPES couldn't exactly ignore it.

"...How did you know?"

"Over the past week, I watched all your TV appearances, back to back to back. And in every one of them, *you moved way too easily for a girl who wears an eye patch.*"

Ordinarily, a person's vision declines by more than 20 percent when they go from seeing out of two eyes to seeing out of one. It's also harder to judge perspective. However, as I watched Saikawa sing and dance, I hadn't seen the slightest suggestion of difficulty.

That wasn't all. On the day we'd gone to her house, she'd held her cup with her left hand as she drank her tea—even though her vision on that side should have been drastically reduced by her eye patch.

When we'd run into each other at the CD store "coincidentally" (she'd probably been watching me), Saikawa had stood on my right. But she wasn't supposed to be able to see out of her left eye, so that had been a really unnatural choice.

In terms of the time line, those hints had started building up early on, and so I'd spent a week thoroughly investigating her.

"Sorry. My old partner taught me to be extra-sensitive to what I saw and heard."

I remembered how, two years ago, Siesta had resolved the Medusa incident at that European mansion in the forest with a *gaze* as her only hint.

...Yeah. It's just like you said, Siesta. Only people with sharp eyes and ears survive in this business.

"...I see. So you never trusted me in the first place, then? Ah-ha-ha. I did wonder what had happened when you told me you desperately wanted to go to the rehearsal."

"Did you think I'd turned into a Yui-nya fan?"

"Yes, I just assumed you'd fallen under my spell."

Yeah, Natsunagi was real suspicious about that, too.

For a moment, Saikawa and I forgot we had each other at gunpoint and snickered a little.

"That man in black yesterday...," Saikawa said. "You engineered that as well, didn't you, Mr. Assistant?"

"You've got good intuition... And, uh, sorry."

I'd wanted actual proof that Saikawa could *see* out of her left eye, so I'd set a trap at that rehearsal. When a crisis hits out of nowhere, people react on instinct.

As the suspicious man had approached her from the left wing of the stage, even though her left eye was covered, Saikawa had seen him clearly.

If she were calm, she might have thought, *I'm not supposed to be able to see out of my left eye, and this man is approaching from my left. I shouldn't notice him.* ...Naturally, that wasn't possible. As a result, Saikawa had screamed before the man managed to reach her, and she had escaped unharmed.

By the way, that man in black had been an acquaintance of mine. Four years ago, he was one of the guys who used to give me attaché cases.

"Really, though, would you normally go to such lengths just to confirm that my left eye had this ability?"

"No, I had one other objective. I wanted a tour of the dome, and the suspicious man provided the perfect excuse. I was hoping to get an idea of the places they were likely to hide today."

"...I think you may have been a little too well prepared."

"It's something my old partner taught me."

What had it been? *"First-rate detectives resolve incidents before they even occur"*?

Although, as the assistant, there was almost no chance I'd ever reach that level.

"Is that about it? Have we both shown all our cards?"

"Let's see... Yes, you've seen all of mine." For the first time in a while, Saikawa gave a charming smile.

Yeah, that's Yui Saikawa, the idol I know.

"All right, now that we're square on that, I'm gonna ask... Would you lower that gun?"

"That's…"

For a moment, Saikawa's face twisted, and she looked down.

"The truth is, I know now… I do. I know you two aren't my enemy. I know you're on my side; I know you're trying to protect me. But."

Again, Saikawa raised her head.

She gave a sad smile, and a single tear traced a line from her right eye.

"But then what am I supposed to do? *How can I protect my left eye?*"

I see. So Saikawa knew, too.

She was aware that killing us wouldn't solve her problem. That the threat wouldn't go away.

After all, SPES wasn't only after me. They'd been keeping Saikawa alive so that she could help get rid of me; now she was in danger as well. That crossbow bolt was incontrovertible proof.

"…I just can't. Mama and Papa are gone. My future is so dark. This eye can see even when there's no light ahead…but without it, I won't make it."

That's not true—that would be so easy to say.

Spending several years in this line of work had given me a way with words.

I already had a smooth reply: *Maybe you can't see what's ahead of you in the darkness, but your fans will hold their glow sticks high and light the way for you.* It would be the easiest thing in the world.

But I knew a bit of wordplay wouldn't save Saikawa.

It had been three years since her parents had died. For three years, she'd done everything she could to keep working as an idol and stay in front of her fans—and still, here she was, holding a gun.

Words weren't what she needed.

Then what *did* she need?

What could save Saikawa?

What did she want most, right now?

It was… It was—

"Hey—once we got all this cleared up, the two of us were planning to go to the beach."

The voice started behind me, but it gradually came up beside me.

"Would you like to come with us?"

The suggestion seemed like the last thing we'd need right now in the midst of this tension.

Saikawa and I had guns pointed at each other's foreheads. Who the hell would talk about going to the beach?

What a detective needs is absolute logic, and occasionally force.

That was how Siesta and I had lived for those three years. We'd fought our way through.

But Natsunagi wasn't like that.

Her essence was—passion.

That was her only weapon—but it was also her strength.

Saikawa stood there with her mouth open, having forgotten both that she was an idol and that she had a gun trained on someone, while Natsunagi went on.

"What I mean is...would you be our friend? That's what I'm trying to say."

The brilliant smile Natsunagi gave to Saikawa would put any idol in the world to shame.

"...How can you say that?" The muzzle of Saikawa's pistol was trembling. "You do understand that I tried to kill both of you, don't you?"

"It's all right," said Natsunagi. "We don't die that easily."

"And I was deceiving you the whole time...," said Saikawa.

"Well, you're an idol singer. Isn't that your job?"

"—! That's not a real argument."

"You're right. I tried to deceive you, too, just now. That means we're even."

"...You're shameless."

"I sure am. So would you accept my shamelessly *selfish request*?" Insisting that this was merely something she personally wanted, Natsunagi gently held out a hand to Saikawa.

Neither I nor Siesta could ever have done it that way.

"That's weird, Miss Natsunagi... It's—it's just..."

"Really? I'm sure being friends with weird people is fun. I discovered that myself recently."

Why did you look at me when you said that, Natsunagi? If anyone's weird here, it's you, all right?

"Even... Even if we were friends...it wouldn't fix anything. And I'd end up causing you all sorts of extra trouble."

"I don't think that's true."

"Huh? Oh—"

Saikawa's trembling had given me a momentary opening, so I took the opportunity to snatch the gun out of her hand.

"Saikawa. You said they were after you, but they're after me, too. Don't think of it as 'trouble.' We're both targets. It would be more convenient to team up."

It was true. Natsunagi's suggestion had sounded ridiculous at first, but I wouldn't have reached that conclusion without her.

If the three of us fought one another, we'd be playing right into the enemy's hands. Instead, we should unite against our common enemy.

I had those three years' worth of *experience*, which had stuck with me whether I wanted it to or not; Natsunagi had her *heart*, with its ultimate courage and DNA; and Saikawa had a *left eye* that saw through everything. We could supplement one another in a lot of ways.

"Then...you'll help me?"

"Yes, we will. So you help us, too, Saikawa."

Sorry—I didn't see it coming, but my life's in danger, too.

Just ten days ago, my life had been so tepid, and yet once I met Natsunagi... and reunited with my former partner...just look at the mess I was in. My trouble magnetism wasn't improving; it was getting worse by the year.

It looked as if I was going to have to fight SPES yet again.

To do that, I needed more people and power than I had now. And so—

"Saikawa, I want you to join us."

And in answer to our simple, plain, naive, intuitive, instinctive attempt to talk her around, Saikawa said—

"—Yes. I'd love to."

I'm positive that innocent smile didn't belong to Yui Saikawa the idol. Right then, she was just a fourteen-year-old girl.

◆ Because you said "Let's go to the beach"

A little over a week after Saikawa's big concert, school let out for summer vacation.

The long (and timely) break was the perfect opportunity for making good on the promise I'd exchanged with Natsunagi and Saikawa. I assumed we'd be going to a beach somewhere nearby, but...

"We're off to the Aegean!"

"That's way too ambitious!"

As the girls cheered and punched the air, psyching themselves up, I was compelled to point out how absurd this was.

"Saikawa, look. Yes, Natsunagi and I suggested that the three of us go to the beach, but how did that turn into an eight-day trip on a boat? What exactly are you imagining when you talk about going to the beach?"

In Japan, you'd usually think of Izu or Shounan or somewhere like that. Why had she jumped to Europe and the Mediterranean...?

Meanwhile, Yui Saikawa—who was wearing a white dress and a big straw hat—just seemed puzzled.

"Huh? But you said we should go, Kimizuka. Besides, the ship's already sailed, so no need to keep harping on it, all right?"

...It was exactly as she said.

We were already out on the ocean, rocked by the waves. The three of us were standing on the deck of a cruise ship, gazing at the receding Japanese archipelago.

"Hear, hear. Nobody likes wishy-washy guys." Natsunagi slipped off her sunglasses and shot me a belligerent look. She was wearing shorts and a baggy T-shirt. Were the spaghetti straps I could see on her shoulders underwear or a swimsuit? Either way, that look was perfect for her. "Anyway. I've never been on a cruise ship, either, so I'm really looking forward to this. Thanks, Yui."

The smile Natsunagi gave Saikawa was the sort she only rarely gave me. After that incident, these two had gotten really close.

"No, no, it's the least I can do to, um, make amends. I can't do much more than this."

She wanted to make amends for putting our lives in danger. Of course, an all-expenses-paid invitation to an ocean voyage on a glamorous cruise ship wasn't enough to make up for that. Saikawa knew it, too. And so—

"You're going to fight SPES with us. As long as you do that, I'll have no complaints."

That had been the promise we'd made—the alliance we'd formed as people whose lives were under threat from the same group.

"Yes, of course. I'll do anything I can."

It felt like both of Saikawa's eyes were gazing right at me—her large, round black one and the sapphire one under her eye patch.

"What's the matter, Kimizuka? Why are you staring at my eyes? ...Ohhh, I know. I've figured it out. Yui-nya's got you for real this time, huh? Well, well, Kimizuka... Heh-heh!" Saikawa folded her arms, nodding away.

Watching this so very genuine, so very simple girl—

"You sure are cute."

—I went and said it.

"Heh-heh! ...Heh-heh, heh...heh?"

At that, Saikawa's proud chuckling ground to a halt. Before long, the upturned corners of her mouth began to twitch uncertainly, and for some reason, her cheeks turned red.

"...U-um. I—I wish you'd be a little more subtle about these things, thank you..."

"Hey, idol, your tolerance should be way higher than that."

So she could dish it out, but she couldn't take it. I'd gotten a glimpse of another side of her—one I didn't really need to know about.

"Time out!"

The next instant, a hand chopped down between Saikawa and me.

"Watch it! Geez, Natsunagi, what was that for?"

"...That was getting a little too rom-and-com for me."

"'Rom-and-com'?"

"Never mind! I have something serious to discuss!" Giving a cute little snort of disdain, Natsunagi folded her arms over her chest. "Why did that

SPES group make contact with Yui now? Seems a little late for that, don't you think?"

"Oh, yes, true," said Saikawa. "That's a good question."

Natsunagi looked at Saikawa, and Saikawa looked at me, tilting her head.

"Why now? Well, I mean…" I was about to say *That's completely obvious*, then thought better of it.

…Yes, come to think of it, it *was* odd.

Saikawa had said she'd gotten that left eye six years ago. If SPES's goal had really been to destroy it, it wouldn't have been strange for them to act sooner… So why had they chosen to do it now?

And Saikawa wasn't the only problem.

Why had SPES waited to start coming after me again?

Over the past year, after Siesta's death, they hadn't shown the slightest bit of interest in me. They'd made the call that they had no time to bother with a lowly, nameless assistant (ouch), so why was I being targeted again now, a year later?

That train of thought naturally led me to a certain deduction.

"…Oh!" Natsunagi gave a small cry, as if she'd realized something.

She might have come to the same conclusion through the process of elimination.

In which case…

"I dunno. There's no telling what goes on in the minds of those lunatics." Giving a faint smile, I punted Natsunagi's unease off the field.

"…You think?"

"Yeah."

After all, this was just a deduction—no more than a theory. I was sure it wasn't the truth.

What if SPES's true target wasn't Saikawa or me, but *Natsunagi, who had Siesta's heart*? Or what if they started getting worried after learning she'd made contact with Siesta's former assistant?

No, that couldn't be it. It shouldn't be.

It was wrong for Natsunagi's life to be destroyed over this.

"Well, we'll just have to accept that we have a big evil organization after us and figure out how to deal." That's why I said something mean-ingless to end the conversation.

But in point of fact, whatever the reason was, after the Saikawa inci-dent, we were definitely even higher on the *"wanted" list* than before. The enemy hadn't shown themselves directly; they'd probably still been watching and waiting—but the upshot was that we'd issued a full declara-tion of war.

The day when I'd have to haul myself out of my tepid life was here.

"Um, so they're hunting for us right now, and we're taking a laid-back cruise..." Natsunagi struck a playful pose. Guess my diplomacy was enough for her.

"Don't go there, Natsunagi."

Still, I got the feeling this was actually the right move. After all, it had worked four years ago.

Back then, Siesta and I had hightailed it out of Japan, leaving on an unforgettable journey with no clear destination. This was probably a reenactment of that day: preordained *fate*.

"Well, ideally, nothing happens," I murmured, and the words drifted away on the sea wind.

No, I know. Really. I know. After all these different coincidences piling up, something was going to happen. We couldn't possibly get off this easy.

Almost immediately, it became obvious that my premonition was correct.

"—Kimizuka?"

Suddenly, someone called to me, and I turned.

Standing there was...

"Charlie...?"

Her natural blond hair streamed in the salt wind, and her neat, clearly European features made even her surprise look beautiful.

"...It's been a year, hasn't it?" I said.

"Yes. It has."

We gazed at each other, our expressions hard.

"Kimizuka, is this a friend of yours?" Natsunagi looked perplexed.

"Yeah, Charlie is my...*our* old comrade."

Charlotte Arisaka Anderson had worshipped the deceased Siesta—and had been her apprentice.

A girl's monologue 2

Kimizuka had given me a new life as an ace detective.

I was no ordinary detective, either. I would be fighting pseudohumans.

…Yet I think I was nervous, somewhere in my mind.

Well, that's no surprise. I was a nobody before this. I couldn't possibly handle such a major role out of the blue. I needed someone else to acknowledge me as the detective, or I wouldn't make it as this new me.

The night I made my resolve to be reborn as someone new—I dreamed about the person who'd once fought the enemies of the world as a real ace detective.

In the dream, Siesta seemed to have a personality that was the complete opposite of mine.

I don't know whether she was really like that, but…from what Kimizuka had told me, I think it was probably about right.

She was logical, and I'm an intuitive type. Polar opposites.

In the dream, we had a huge fight, which turned physical, and it was a hideous, ugly mess.

But I won, in the end. (Well, it's technically possible that Siesta took the high road and withdrew, but I'm not going to try to find out. Mostly for the sake of my honor.) Ultimately, Siesta said she'd entrust Kimizuka to me. (I mean, it wasn't like we were fighting over him, but I'm not going to get into the details. Mostly for the sake of Siesta's honor.)

I'm kinda making it into a joke, but it meant so much to me.

Now I can become an ace detective in both name and fact.

I can finally *be* somebody.

—But that also means I'm not allowed to fail.

I hated being nobody. I don't want to go back to when there was nothing.

Anything but that *darkness*. Never again.

One day, one year ago

"Ma'am! Why do I have to buddy up with a guy like him?!"

The small rocking boat was already unpleasant, and her shrill voice was making my headache worse.

There were three of us on deck.

Me, Siesta, and Charlie, who'd been pestering and wailing like a little kid for a while now.

We were crossing the ocean, on our way to accomplish a certain objective...but we seemed to have hit a snag right off the bat.

"I'd rather throw myself into the sea right this minute than work with Kimizuka as a partner!"

She's really running me down...but I'm used to it. I've literally never seen this girl in a good mood. "It's just a temporary maneuver, Charlie," I said.

Meanwhile, Siesta (or Ma'am, according to Charlie) spoke as coolly as ever. "You've been on several similar maneuvers before, remember?"

"Yeah, and I hated it every time!"

"Is that right?"

"Yes!"

"I had no idea."

As the rough sea rocked the boat, Siesta took a sip of her black tea with a gentle tip of the cup. I was detecting a hint of mockery in the gesture.

"Until *he* showed up, *I* was your partner, Ma'am." Charlie shot me a sharp glare.

Ooh, scary. I'm afraid.

"Partners? She only assigned you jobs every so often, right?" I shot back.

"Ngh..." Charlie looked down, embarrassed. "B-but still. I...was

Ma'am's first apprentice..." To show her respect, Charlie even used "Ma'am" in place of Siesta's name.

Charlotte Arisaka Anderson was about my age, a girl with roots in both America and Japan.

Charlie's parents were in the army, and she'd been given a strict upbringing. She'd spent time in a variety of organizations, and even as young as she was, she'd already completed multiple military missions. One of those had involved combat with SPES, and she'd joined our team frequently, on Siesta's request.

Her position could have been "security," "spy," or "soldier."

However, if you asked her, *"Siesta's apprentice"* was the one that fit best.

"Yes. You're right, Charlie. You've saved me many times. Thank you for all you've done."

"Ma'am...!"

"Come here."

Charlie ran up to Siesta's knees and nuzzled against her like a puppy. Siesta stroked her blond hair gently, combing it with her fingers.

"Heh-heh." Charlie looked bashful and contented. Gradually, her eyes turned toward me. "......Heh!"

"Uh, I'm not jealous."

Why was she looking so smug? What was wrong with her?

"Well, it would certainly make my life easier if you two would get along a little better," Siesta murmured, smiling wryly, after she'd stroked Charlie's head for a while.

"Oh! That's right!" Charlie sprang up from Siesta's lap. "I still haven't agreed to work with Kimizuka!"

Apparently, Siesta's fingers on her hair had made her forget all about it.

"Don't give Siesta too much trouble, Charlie," I said. "We don't have much time left."

"...I'd appreciate it if you didn't call me by my nickname."

She cares about that now?

I swear, she's a total kid beneath that grown-up exterior. Does she resent me that much for taking Siesta from her? ...I mean, not that she's actually mine or anything, but still.

"Listen to me. Neither of you is perfect." Siesta admonished us, getting

the situation under control again. "That's why you need to work together and compensate for your individual weaknesses."

"My weaknesses...? I can't think of anything in particular."

"Are you stupid, Kimi?"

There it was: the line Siesta said all the time when I did something wrong.

"You can't eat green peas, and you have a harder time waking up on winter mornings than I do. You always make a face when you take medicine, and you try to avoid roads that have pigeons or crows on them even if it means taking the long way around. Can you still say you have no weaknesses?"

"...I don't think I've ever told you anything about any of that."

"I don't need you to tell me to know that much. We're together enough."

Oh yeah? Well, stop there, all right? Charlie's getting grumpy.

"So? What does this have to do with role division?"

"Yes. You're clever, but if you got in a fight with a water flea, you'd probably lose. You're completely unsuited to combat."

"...I am, huh?"

Getting a bad feeling, I glanced over at Charlie. She was watching me and snickering.

"Meanwhile, Charlie..."

"Yes?!"

"You have solid skills in battle, but you're not the brightest bulb."

"What?!"

"Pfft! Snrk, snrk."

"—I heard that laugh, Kimizuka! You just laughed at me, didn't you?! I'll kill you! I will shoot you dead right now!"

"No fighting. You're better than that."

"Ow!"

"Wah!"

Siesta karate-chopped each of us on the head. *Dammit, I'm not the bad guy here.*

"I want you to get through this maneuver by working together."

"This maneuver" was the recovery of a *comrade* who was being held prisoner on a certain island that was effectively under the control of SPES. Failure was definitely not an option.

"But, Ma'am, that means you'll be by yourself..." Charlie's worry was only natural.

If she and I buddied up, Siesta would be forced to act on her own.

"Don't underestimate me, please," Siesta replied. "I'm ten times the fighter you are, Charlie. I'm also a hundred times smarter than my assistant. There's no call for you to worry about me."

I got the feeling my evaluation had been unfairly low, but whatever. During this maneuver, I'd make it clear just how smart I was. She'd have to revise her opinion then.

Maybe it was because I was making stupid plans instead of doing something more worthwhile.

"That being the case, I want the two of you to get along with each other. Now, and from now on."

That was the day the ace detective died.

Chapter 3

◆ Yesterday's enemy is today's enemy, too

"I didn't think we'd be seeing each other again after all this time, Kimizuka."

We were on the deck of a luxury cruise ship.

The individual who'd interrupted my conversation with Natsunagi and Saikawa was Charlotte Arisaka Anderson—and it was the first time I'd seen her in a year, since the day Siesta died.

"Yeah, it surprised me, too. How've you been?"

"You have no reason to be concerned about my health."

Oh yeah? Well, good to see you haven't changed a bit.

I thought I'd fire back with a lighthearted jab, but—

"...Really, what on earth have you been doing all this time?"

Suddenly, Charlie's tone came down a step, and there was a sharp light in her large eyes.

"'All this time'?"

"Since she died." Charlie bit her lip. She was as beautiful as ever, but her expression was harder than it used to be.

"What have I been doing...? Nothing, actually." Thinking back over this past year, I answered honestly.

I could have said I'd done something, but only very recently. After I met Natsunagi.

"Yes, I imagine not," Charlie answered derisively, as if she'd been expecting that answer. "You caught bag snatchers, went around searching for lost dogs and cats, received commendations from your local police... And you think that makes you a hero?"

Oh, so she knew, huh? She knew about my tepid life.

"Kimizuka—didn't you have any intention of inheriting Ma'am's job?"

...I see. So that was what she'd wanted to say all along, huh? She'd been checking into what I was doing this past year because she wanted to say that. I seemed to remember Ms. Fuubi saying something similar to me at one point.

However, my answer to that was:

"For those three years, I was just the assistant. All I can do is *assist*."

And the one I was meant to assist was gone. I was powerless.

"...That's right. You were her assistant, Kimizuka. Her only assistant. So..." The sea wind carried her whisper far away. Charlie's long eyelashes came down slowly, as if she was thinking about something. "Well? What are you doing here, then? Changed your mind?"

By the time Charlie asked me that question, she'd reverted to her usual firm expression.

"What am I doing here? Uh, I'm on a cruise."

"...I see. You don't even know." Charlie gave a disgusted sigh. "So it's only a coincidence that you're on this ship."

"...Is there something here?"

I glanced at Saikawa, but she shook her head emphatically. Apparently, she had no idea what this was about.

"Ma'am's last wish."

"Huh?"

"Just before she died, in order to bring down SPES, she left her last wish—her legacy—all over the world. One piece of it is dormant somewhere on this cruise ship. The analysis took time, but that information is sound," Charlie said. "Although the analysis team isn't part of my organization."

I remembered that part of the work wasn't exactly her forte. Siesta had teased her about it quite a lot. Still—

"Siesta's legacy is on this ship...?"

And Charlie was here to search for it.

And today, by coincidence, I just happened to be on the same boat.

Coincidence? Really?

"But since you have no intention of carrying out Ma'am's dying wish, it's none of your business. You can just rot in your tepid life forever." With that, Charlie turned to go.

"No, hang on a second. Charlie..."

"I'm not who I was a year ago," she said. "I'm not the girl who couldn't save Ma'am."

With that, Charlie told me good-bye...well, told her past self good-bye, in all likelihood.

"*I* inherited that last wish."

The voice that rang out then was clear and carrying, the sort that traveled all the way to distant islands.

Natsunagi stepped out in front of me, facing Charlie straight on.

"And you are?"

"I'm Nagisa Natsunagi—the ace detective."

This was getting dangerous; I could almost see the sparks flying.

"Nagisa Natsunagi...?" Charlie said quietly, putting a hand to her chin, and then—

"Oh, you're the..."

Her eyes went to Natsunagi's heart. That had to be one of the most important items of information linked to Siesta. Had Charlie tracked that down as well?

"I don't suppose you'd want to play detective somewhere else, would you? I don't want to see you using Ma'am's life for a game of pretend," Charlie said frostily, with obvious irritation in her eyes.

"I'm not playing!" Nagisa shot back, setting her hand over the left side of her chest. "I was given this life, and that has to mean something! Siesta entrusted it to me! And so, I'll be the one to find that legacy—I swear on this heart!"

She'd snapped at me like this once, too; it was fierce and fiery, a declaration of war.

For a moment, Charlie's eyes went wide, as if Natsunagi had overwhelmed her.

"—I see. Do whatever you want," she said, promptly turning on her heel. "There's no way you could ever replace her. I'll be the one to inherit her last wish."

As I watched her receding back, I couldn't think of anything to say.

"Aw, she left..."

Finally, Saikawa spoke up. Maybe she didn't want the mood to get too heavy.

"Um, I'm sorry," she continued. "If I hadn't invited you two onto this ship, this would never have..."

"No, it's not your fault, Saikawa." I immediately rejected that idea. I couldn't let my personal situation spoil Saikawa's gesture of kindness. "It was more like, you know, a collision of really unfortunate coincidences," I said, partly to convince myself as well. "You too, Natsunagi. I'm sorry for pulling you into all that."

"......"

"...Natsunagi?"

When I looked at her, her fists were clenched, her shoulders were trembling, and...

"Nnnnnnnngggggghhhhhhh! Gaaaaaaaaaaaaaaaaaaaaaaaah!"

...her face turned bright red, and she started pounding her knees with her fists, again and again.

"Kimizuka, do you think this is a greeting from abroad, perhaps?"

"No idea... Makes me think of a gorilla more than anything, but..."

"A gorilla, hmm? Did you know their official scientific name is *Gorilla gorilla gorilla*...?"

"Yeah. And all of them have type B blood..."

"Would you shut up about gorillas?!"

Finally, the gorilla—er, Natsunagi, whose face was as red as an apple, launched into an angry diatribe at someone who had already left.

"Arrrrgh, what a *jerk*! I'm playing *pretend*, huh?! I... Just how does she think I felt when I...!"

Yeah, I know. I know you're serious.

If anyone was wrong back there, it was me.

I'd been Siesta's only assistant, and I had failed to carry out my role. Not to mention I didn't even want to inherit her last wish.

No wonder Charlie'd had it with me. I was the one who deserved the blame, not Natsunagi.

"I am going to be the one who finds it. *Her* legacy. Count on it," Natsunagi said, as I'd suspected she would. Her eyes were narrowed, and her fists were tightly clenched.

"I think you're getting a little too worked up about this."

"Huh...? You...think so...?"

"Why don't you go cool off in the pool? We've got time for that. Right, Saikawa?"

"......! Yes! There's even a waterslide!"

Of course there was; this was a luxury cruise ship owned by the Saikawa family. Natsunagi's swimsuit purchase was about to pay off.

"Are you coming, too, Kimizuka?"

"Uh, I'm..." I gave it a little thought. "Sorry. There's something I need to do."

Yeah. The one who really needed to cool down was me.

"...I see." Natsunagi's shoulders drooped a little, but she didn't try to get any details out of me. She signaled to Saikawa, and they both turned to go.

"See you later, then."

"All right, Kimizuka. I'm gonna burn the sight of Nagisa onto my retinas!"

"...Yui, actually, maybe let's not go into the pool together, okay?"

◆ Welcome to hell, the land of dreams

For a little while after Natsunagi and Saikawa had left for the pool, I stayed on deck, thinking.

I met an enemy (comrade) of mine again after a year. It would have been easy to call this encounter a coincidence.

But I knew we were in too deep for that.

Natsunagi had taught me as much during the incident with her heart—you can't just brush off people's feelings or your reunions with them. The word *coincidence* is too irresponsible and fatalistic.

I had to assume that every meeting and reunion in this recent chain of events meant something. Reaching that conclusion, I knew where I should be going next.

After all, what I had to do now was talk things out with the right person. As for where I'd find her... Well, we'd known each other long enough that I could pretty much guess.

I made my way through the vast ship, opened a door that was larger than the rest, and—

"Ha-ha. Ah, memories."

The first thing I saw was long rows of slot machines. Toward the rear, there were green tables where you could play roulette and baccarat, with dealers running the games.

This place was magnificent and debauched, a seething mass of human desires, a paradise of dreams, or hell itself—a casino.

Casinos were illegal in Japan, but once you were out on the ocean, that law no longer applied.

...Still, this really did take me back.

Las Vegas, Macao, Singapore—a few years ago, when I'd been traveling all over the world with Siesta, I'd learned to gamble. On the occasional days when we'd used what little money we had to win big, Siesta and I had lived it up.

Speaking of "living it up," there was one day when we both drank liquor—something neither of us did as a rule—and got pretty drunk, and then... No, actually, I won't tell that story. I'm sure it happened because we were, you know, young and thoughtless.

Past stories aside, the important thing now was whether *she* was here, and...yep, there she was.

"Ngh, why...? That's my seventeenth loss in a row. Nobody else is losing..." She was slumped over a poker table, the blond hair she was so proud of comically disheveled. "Urgh, this just can't be right. One more time... One more time!"

Apparently having failed to learn her lesson, she took a twenty-dollar bill out of her wallet, intending to have the dealer convert it into chips for her.

"What are you doing, you moron?"

Seriously, I can't just stand by and watch this. I landed a karate chop on that blond head.

"Wh-who's there?" Her shoulders flinched, and then she turned awkwardly to look at me.

"What kind of idiot gambles herself to tears?"

Charlie was sitting there, her eyes watery and pained. "Nnnnngh! Kimizuka, I can't win…"

"What happened to all that spirit you had when you were picking a fight with us?"

Well, Charlie always had been like this.

When the talk turned to Siesta, she tended to forget herself, but generally, she acted her age… Actually, her mature looks only made her childish moments more prominent. Frankly, she was kinda unreliable—and to borrow Siesta's words, not the brightest bulb.

…I didn't say it, all right? Siesta did.

"Why are you messing around with poker?"

"…Well, they say this is Ma'am's *legacy*, so I thought if I kept winning at the casino, it might, you know, turn up as a prize or something…"

"I see. Good to see you're still dim as ever."

Although, thanks to that, I did manage to guess where she'd be right away.

"What's that supposed to mean?!"

"It means Siesta was really seeing you."

"Huh?! Ma'am really saw me? …Heh-heh."

Don't give me that "heh-heh" business. One second she's crying, then she's mad, then she's laughing… Seriously, there's always something going on with her.

"Switch with me a sec."

"Huh?"

I took Charlie's place in front of the young female dealer. "I'll win back what you lost, at least."

"…A-and what are you going to ask me for in return?" Charlie backed away, hugging herself. *This is why people say you're stupid.*

"I'll settle for a conversation."

"…Conversation?"

"Later. We'll go back out on deck." I handed the dealer a twenty. "Just watch. I've always had a knack for poker."

I'll show that ace detective, wherever she is, the difference between you and me.

◆ That's why I can't be a detective

"—I can't believe you lost."

As I stood on the deck, staring vacantly at the ocean, someone was snarking at me from the vicinity of my knees, in a tone that would ordinarily be unthinkable.

Charlie leaned against the railing with her back to me. "What the heck was that? You stroll in like 'Oh, I'm so cool, I've always had a knack for poker' and then you go and lose?" Charlie was sitting on the deck, hugging her knees. She looked up at me teasingly.

"Oh, shut up. I just sort of thought I could pull it off, okay?"

Long story short, I got destroyed at the casino.

Humans have a hopeless tendency to see the past through rose-colored glasses. When I thought back carefully, I remembered that it had been Siesta, not me, who'd won big at the casino with that knack for poker. I'd only been granted her leftovers… That's one hell of a trap.

"That is beyond pathetic. Not only that, but you got sucked in even worse than I did and blew all the money you had. Talk about stupid. Talk about *sick.*"

"I already feel terrible, so don't pour salt in the wound, thanks."

Haaaah. Maybe I'll borrow money from Natsunagi when she gets back from the pool. Swallow my pride, et cetera.

No, this was a time to ask Saikawa. Everybody should have a rich friend.

"Heh-heh. But yes, you were right," Charlie said. "That was pretty funny."

Was it actually a joke all along?

Charlie gave a contrived-sounding laugh. "Pfft! Snrk, snrk."

Come to think of it, it was the first time in a year that I'd seen that smile.

For a little while, we laughed together quietly.

"—So? What did you want to talk about?"

The wind blew, changing the peaceful atmosphere.

"Siesta." As I answered, I rested my arms on the boat's railing and gazed out to sea.

"...We already had that conversation. It's over."

"Says you. Communication is a game of catch, you know." Up till now, my conversations with Charlie had always been more like dodgeball.

"What could I possibly have to talk about, a year later, with Ma'am's assistant, who didn't try to carry out her last wish?" Charlie's voice was cold again.

Unsurprisingly, that was something she just couldn't compromise on. I'd been chosen as Siesta's assistant, and then after she'd died, I hadn't tried to carry on her legacy. I'd averted my eyes from the beings I should have been fighting and stayed in my lukewarm life.

And I was the one who hated myself the most for all of it.

Yes. I bet that's why Charlie was—

"I'm sorry. I didn't mean to worry you," I said.

She'd been concerned about me, her enemy—her comrade—all this time.

"...I'd like it if you wouldn't presume to know what I'm thinking."

"You even read all those newspaper articles about me."

"I—I just happened to see them; that's all."

"And then you came all this way, just to see me."

"I told you that was a coincidence!"

"Ow!"

Charlie's fist sank into my lower thigh... I guess I teased her a little too much. But really, I probably had worried her. I did feel bad about that.

"Still," she said, "since you *did* apologize, I'll give you one chance."

"Oh yeah?"

Charlie got to her feet and came to stand beside me. "Why didn't you try to become a detective in Ma'am's place?" Her eyes shone like emeralds, and they wouldn't let me get away. It was too late to lie or pull a fast one.

"...She... Siesta said something to me."

I remembered what had happened on that day, four years ago. In the sky, at ten thousand meters.

On the plane that Bat had hijacked, Siesta told me—

"You—be my assistant."

That was what she'd said.

"That's why I can't be a detective. I couldn't four years ago. I can't now that she's dead, either. I'm sure I'll never be able to. I'll always be hers: the ace detective's assistant."

I can't be her. But I can continue to live for her.

"...Dummy." The corners of Charlie's lips curved up in a way that looked a little sad. "You're the one who's stuck in the past with Ma'am, not me."

Was that true? Maybe so.

Even now, I'm sure. Siesta is my—

"Well, it doesn't matter." Charlie smiled, then looked up ahead, far out to sea. "You should find Ma'am's legacy, and your own answer, your way. Because I'm planning to do it my way." Charlie pressed her lips together tight.

I swallowed the "Thank you" threating to escape me and went for a grateful-sounding "Sorry" instead. "Her legacy, huh...?" Once again, I started to think about what Siesta had apparently left on this ship. "If your team got that information, Charlie, the enemy might have it, too... You think it's possible?"

"You mean SPES?"

"Yeah."

When it came to information warfare, they gave as good as they got. On top of that, Siesta had been one of their greatest enemies. If they knew she'd laid the groundwork for something, they were bound to try to...

"It is a definite possibility. Well, I do technically have an idea, but..."

"A-an idea? *You* have an idea, Charlie...?"

"...I see you're desperate to *fight* me," Charlie said, flashing the holster she wore on her hip.

What did it mean that all the girls I'd met lately carried handguns?

"I told you, remember? I'm not who I was a year ago." The way she was puffing up was still more or less the same, though. "Oh, speaking of that. Kimizuka, starting today, let me borrow your cabin."

"Huh? Why? If you're part of the tour, you've got your own."

"I have nothing of the sort." Charlie tilted her head, straight-faced. "After all, I'm a stowaway."

"Don't give me that!"

Come to think of it, she was particularly good at covert maneuvers… *C'mon, just pay the money. Don't use it to gamble.*

"Give me the key to your cabin."

"That's not fair at all. Actually, how did you get onto the boat? Did you use optical camouflage?"

"Heh-heh. Industry secret."

For some reason, Charlie seemed extremely proud of this. She was puffing her chest out so far I wondered if her shirt would split open, so I wished she wouldn't stop.

"Optical camouflage, hmm…?" Charlie put a hand to her chin and murmured softly. Thanks to her mature looks, the pensive expression really suited her. Although for as long as I could remember, that face usually meant she was thinking *What should I have for dinner tonight…?* or something along those lines, so it wasn't much help.

"Listen, Kimizuka?"

Abruptly, Charlie looked up and asked:

"Do you suppose there's a way to get off this ship in the middle of the ocean?"

◆ Cinderella before midnight

After I'd parted ways with Charlie and her incomprehensible question, I met up with Natsunagi and Saikawa, who'd returned from the pool.

After that, the three of us explored the vast ship together, searching for "Siesta's legacy"…but we had no idea what we were even trying to find. Naturally, our search didn't go well.

While we were busy, the sun went down, so we decided to have dinner

もぐ

もぐ

MOGU MOGU
(NOM NOM)

in the restaurant. The tour's guest of honor, Saikawa, was busy making the rounds and greeting everyone, so Natsunagi and I were the only ones who got to eat.

"This feels kind of weird." Natsunagi was using her knife and fork to cut up her salmon meunière in the ship's French restaurant.

"What does?"

"Sitting across from you and eating dinner together like this."

"You don't want to?"

"You know I didn't say that."

Even filled with reproach, her eyes were remarkably cute. How nice it would be if her personality got just a little cuter, too.

"Then what?" I said. "Are you saying that having dinner alone together is almost like a date?"

"…It takes real guts to say that when you're flat broke."

"I have no excuses to give there."

If it hadn't been for Saikawa's kindness, I wouldn't even have been able to pay for our meals here, and I'd probably have spent the rest of my life on this boat working off my debt. Gambling is a terrifying thing.

Speaking of gambling, should I fill her in on what happened with Charlie earlier? This morning, the two of them ended up goading each other into a fight, but I should probably tell her Charlie isn't really all that bad.

"Natsunagi, do you have time after this?"

"Huh? Um, I don't have anything planned. I'm just gonna shower, then go to bed."

"I see. In that case, there's a little something I'd like to talk about."

"Talk? We could just do that here…"

"Uh, the subject's a little hard to discuss in a place like this." SPES would come up as well, and we'd be touching on some sensitive stuff. I'd rather do that away from so many eyes. "There was a bar across the way, wasn't there? Can I ask you to meet me there in an hour?"

"Ummm… Me, by myself? Alone with you?"

"Yeah."

This was really something I should fill Saikawa in on, too, but she was busy being the guest of honor right now, so it would keep.

"I—I see. So you want to talk, alone with me, at a bar…and tell me something you don't want other people to hear..." Natsunagi's lips were moving; she was mumbling. She was looking down and, for some reason, blushing. "W-well, all right... Okay, so I'll see you in an hour."

She speared her remaining meunière with her fork, crammed it into her mouth all at once, got up, and trotted away. What the hell was that about?

"The main course isn't even here yet," I called after her.

I'd really rather have given the extra food to Charlie, but she was probably relaxing in my cabin by now. She couldn't actually have found a way off the ship.

"Well, if we'd had dinner alone together, we'd have nothing to talk about."

Over the course of an hour, I somehow managed to finish a multicourse meal for two by myself. Then I headed for the bar where we'd promised to meet.

"...Sorry to keep you waiting."

When I'd been sitting at the table for a little while, Natsunagi came in, right on time. To avoid being noticed, I'd chosen a spot away from the counter; we were in one of the booths in the back, facing each other across the table.

...Even so.

"You changed clothes for this?"

"Huh? Oh, no, it just, um, happened? After I took a shower, this was all I had to wear."

Natsunagi's outfit was a dramatic change from the casual clothes she'd been in before. She was wearing a low-cut dress, with a thin shawl around her shoulders.

I mean, yeah, it was an appropriate way to dress for this place... But she'd taken more care with her makeup than usual, and I caught the scent of perfume. Was this why she'd hurried back to her room like that? So she could get ready?

"Haaah, well, you can wear whatever you want."

"Whatever...?" Natsunagi pouted, looking a little cross. Had I said something wrong? "And? Um, the talk..."

"Oh, right. Well, let's drink while we talk."

The drinks I'd ordered before Natsunagi got here had just arrived.

"Is it alcoholic?" she asked.

"No, Cinderella."

"Me?"

"The drink."

I'd ordered her a nonalcoholic cocktail by that name. For myself, I'd gotten a Shirley Temple, another famous virgin cocktail. I was sick of alcohol-fueled mistakes.

"All right, just listen for a little while."

After we drank a toast, I began to tell her about Charlie as a person, including how I'd met her.

"This was not what I thought it was going to be." Once I'd finished my story, Natsunagi seemed to wilt a little. "...Well, I mean, this isn't *that*... It's just the influence of the heart's owner, that's all..."

"What are you muttering about?"

"—! ...Huh? What?" she said, suddenly irritated.

"Huh? Why did you just snap out of nowhere?"

"I didn't snap."

"No, you totally did."

"I'm telling you, I didn't!" The toe of her high heel connected with my shin. "I'll double-kill you!"

"That's not fair!"

—Getting back on topic.

"Anyway. I see what you mean. She's not as awful as I thought she was." As Natsunagi spoke, she took a sip of her cocktail. "Siesta was always on her mind, and she still is, even now. She's so genuine it's a little inspiring."

"Yeah. She's genuinely dumb. Sometimes what she says and does is out there, but that might be one of the best things about her." Although I'd die before I told her that.

"You're right... To be honest, I knew it, too."

"That Charlie wasn't a bad person, you mean?"

"That, too, but...the fact that I was in the wrong." With a troubled smile, Natsunagi went on. "The things she said were right on the mark."

She must have been talking about their argument that morning. Charlie had told Natsunagi to quit playing detective. And Natsunagi had just admitted that she was doing just that.

"I didn't spend a long time with Siesta the way Charlie did, and I don't have any strengths I'm really proud of. All I have is this heart...and the *belief* that I've inherited her last wish." Her voice dropped to a self-deprecating murmur in the quiet bar. "I do know that much."

She was right. As Natsunagi herself admitted, she and Siesta were different in many ways.

The color of their hair, of course. The way they spoke, their personalities, their principles, and even the way they carried themselves.

Natsunagi could never become a Siesta doll. And yet—

"What made you decide you'd accept Siesta's role?"

That day—the day when we'd learned that Natsunagi's transplanted heart had belonged to Siesta—Natsunagi had decided to become an ace detective. Even when I'd told her she didn't have to replace anyone, she'd chosen to take that path.

But I still hadn't really heard her thoughts on the matter. I'd decided her silence was something I should respect, and I'd looked the other way. But it was probably time to wake up. For both of us.

"The thing is—I've had poor health ever since I was little." Natsunagi narrowed her eyes, remembering the distant past. "While everyone around me was going to school, I was stuck in bed, all alone. My only friends were some picture books and a little teddy bear. When I saw idols singing and dancing on TV, I was so, so jealous of them."

In my mind's eye, I saw a white hospital room, filled with the smell of chemicals, and a young girl with an IV drip in her thin arm.

"I used to think, *I'll never go anywhere. I'll never get to leave this room.* I couldn't study, couldn't exercise. I was sure I'd never be anyone." Natsunagi smiled, but I could see a hint of tears in her eyes. "It was really scary. But time passed, and then I flew out of my cage. I was given a new life; after that, I had no choice but to test out my wings. Only...I didn't know how to fly."

"How to fly?"

"Yeah… How to live. So I think I wanted an *axis*."

An axis, to help her live her life.

When Natsunagi said that word, I realized it was probably the core of our entire conversation.

"I wasn't anybody, and then all of a sudden, I had to be. So I relied on this heart… I decided to model my approach to life on hers."

These were the true feelings she'd kept hidden inside.

This was why she'd listened to the voice of that heart. She'd pursued the person the heart was looking for, "X"—me—and had taken up the role of ace detective.

It had happened during the Saikawa incident as well. At first, I'd been planning on turning down the request, but Natsunagi had given a random reason to make us take it. Now I could understand the logic behind her unnatural proactiveness.

Natsunagi could only find her way in life by using the ace detective—Siesta—as her axis. And that was just as true of me.

"So it's exactly as Charlie said. I've been playing detective this whole time. I know this is only make-believe."

"Natsunagi…" I tried to say something to her, but the words wouldn't come out right.

…Because we were the same.

I had the same complex she did, and I didn't know what I should do from here on out. Which meant that right now, I had no answers to give her.

"I'm sorry. I'm going to call it a night." Draining the rest of her cocktail in one gulp, Natsunagi stood up.

"Natsunagi, I…"

"Good night. See you tomorrow, okay?" As Natsunagi waved at me, her expression was no different from usual. That was how I knew this conversation was over.

"Yeah, see you tomorrow." All I could do was watch her small back get farther and farther away. "'See you tomorrow,' huh…?"

That's right—this isn't over yet.

I'd have to get my thoughts together and watch for a chance to talk about it again. For now, I decided to head back to my cabin...except Charlie took it over, didn't she? If I tried quietly slipping into the bed with her, I'd probably wake up dead tomorrow.

Well, that left only one option. I took out my phone.

"Uh, hello, Saikawa?"

"Yes, speaking... What is it? It's kinda late, isn't it?"

"Are you in your cabin already? Sorry, but could you let me stay there tonight?"

While I was there, I'd tell her about Charlie and what I'd just discussed with Natsunagi.

"...I'll put on some cute undies while I'm waiting."

"What is wrong with you?"

◆ The worst happens

The next morning, the commotion outside the cabin woke me up.

"Urk, ngh... What's going on...?"

"Nnnnngh, be quiet...Kimizuka..."

"...Nn. Hey, stop. Let go of me, Saikawa."

Untangling myself from Saikawa, who was hugging my arm, I sluggishly sat up.

"What the heck is all the noise about...?" Joints cracking and popping, I stepped into the corridor, and...

"What the hell was that announcement?! Whose voice was that?!"

"I don't know! I don't see any signs that someone got into the radio room, but..."

For some reason, there were crew members running around in a panic.

"Kimizukaaaa...?"

"Hey, Saikawa, look alive. Something's wrong."

Saikawa came over to me, rubbing sleep-dazed eyes. I was urging her to go wash her face, when—

"Attention all passengers."

—an announcement in a creepy, synthesized voice echoed through the ship's corridors.

"We have a girl with us in the lounge."

Was this about a lost kid? Under most normal circumstances, that would have been the case. But from the way the crew members were reacting, this wasn't an official broadcast.

That meant—

"The girl's name is—Nagisa Natsunagi."

""......!"""

Saikawa and I looked at each other. I had an awful feeling about this, and I knew it wasn't just a feeling.

"If this rings a bell with anyone, please hurry to the fifth-floor lounge."

"Saikawa... This is *what I think it is*, isn't it?"

"...Yes. I think *the worst* is happening."

"We have a girl with us."

If this wasn't about a lost child, I could think of only one possibility.

That girl, Nagisa Natsunagi, had been kidnapped.

"See you tomorrow": The words she'd said when we parted last night played in my ears, over and over.

First, Saikawa and I went to Natsunagi's cabin and confirmed that it was empty, then headed for the lounge mentioned in the announcement, the one on the fifth-floor deck.

When we got to the entrance, it had already been closed off by ship security, and an inspection was underway inside.

"Was Miss Natsunagi there?" Saikawa asked a security guard. As the owner of this ship, she had the right to know everything.

"No. Crew members came running immediately after the announcement, but they found nothing."

The guard shot a glance at me, because I looked like an outsider, but Saikawa gave a small nod to indicate that I belonged.

"...That being the case, we haven't found anyone who appears to be the *criminal* yet, either."

"I see..." Saikawa looked down, apparently thinking hard.

...Dammit, what's going on?

We'd followed instructions and come here, but we couldn't even find Natsunagi, much less her kidnapper.

"For now, go over the passenger list carefully. Then check all the cabins and compare the faces and names."

"Understood, miss."

Saikawa issued instructions to the security guard, searching for a clue that could get us somewhere.

She was right. This was a cruise ship, out on the ocean. Even if there was a criminal, he couldn't possibly have gone anywhere else. Natsunagi had to be on the ship somewhere.

…*Hmm? A way to get off this ship…?*

"Hey, Saikawa." I waited until the security guard had left his post, then asked my host, "Is there any way to get off this boat in the middle of the cruise?" Excluding regularly scheduled ports of call, of course.

"Huh? Charlie asked me that same question yesterday."

"Yesterday? You talked with Charlie before I went to your cabin last night?"

"Yes, in the evening. She came to see me."

What? When did that happen…? "And? Did you tell her?"

"Yes, well. I mentioned the lifeboats."

I see. Of course the ship would have those. So had Charlie really left the ship? *If so, don't tell me… Did she take Natsunagi along?*

No, I had to be overthinking it. Charlie had absolutely no motive for grabbing Natsunagi and jumping ship.

"…Actually, Saikawa, why did you help Charlie?" Speaking of motives, I couldn't think of a single reason for Saikawa to side with her…

"Heh-heh. Didn't you know, Kimizuka? Looking through solid objects isn't the only thing this eye can do." Saikawa touched the patch covering her left eye with her fingertips. At first glance, that didn't seem to have anything to do with this situation, but…this definitely wasn't idle rambling. "For one thing, it can also see whether someone is telling a lie or saying what they really feel."

"It can…?"

"Yes. And last night, when Charlie came to see me, she didn't tell a single lie. She said there was something she had to do, which was why she had to get off this ship immediately."

That did sound like the sort of thing Charlie would say.

"I'm planning to do it my way."

It probably meant Charlie had an idea, and she had made a move before I had.

"So I decided to help her just a little. After all, when a girl's in trouble, I can't just leave her there."

I suspected this story might be a white lie on Saikawa's part. I really couldn't believe that her sapphire eye had the ability to read minds. But Saikawa was probably doing the *job* she believed was right, in her own way.

"...Still, why didn't you tell me about it? I don't mind if you helped Charlie out, but you could have mentioned it to me, couldn't you?" *I even stayed in your room last night because I thought Charlie had taken mine.*

"What? Well, I mean, if I'd told you, you wouldn't have spent the night in my room, would you, Kimizuka?"

"That was the goal there?!" *No, seriously, what was she after...?*

"Heh-heh! Just kidding. Did I make your heart skip a beat?"

Then she gave an exaggerated wink with her right eye.

...I swear. Unlike you, I don't have the ability to detect lies. Gimme a break.

But the tension had softened a bit. The next thing I knew, both my nervous sweat and the crease between my eyebrows had vanished. Maybe that was one of Yui Saikawa's idol skills.

"Miss Saikawa!" Just then, a security guard came running toward us from the lounge. "This was discovered on one of the counter seats inside."

He was holding a book. The title was—

"*The Memoirs of Sherlock Holmes*," Saikawa murmured softly.

I knew that book. It was a collection of short stories by Arthur Conan Doyle, detailing the exploits of the legendary detective.

I took the book from the security guard and flipped through the pages... and a bookmark fell out. The page it had been marking was in the short story "The Adventure of the *Gloria Scott*," a tale of the event that had led Holmes to become a detective. A ship had also sunk in that story.

The bookmark had a message on it:

At 8:00 PM, come to the main deck with the ace detective's legacy.

◆ How to use a three-billion-yen family treasure

"Not here, either…"

"Nope, guess not. Let's move on."

Feeling a little dejected, Saikawa and I left the sit-down restaurant we'd been searching and headed for the next location.

At the moment, we were walking around the ship on a search. Instead of Siesta's legacy, we were looking for Natsunagi herself.

"Dammit. So cheating isn't gonna cut it, huh?"

"I'm using my left eye, so I really don't think we could have missed anything, but…"

"Yeah…you're right." My fingernails bit into my palms. If the pain stimulated my brain, so much the better.

I was thinking about the message on that bookmark. The criminal had demanded that we give them Siesta's legacy if we wanted to save Natsunagi's life.

But we had no idea what that legacy was. The previous day, Charlie had told us only that something along those lines apparently existed, and we didn't yet know what it was, specifically. Charlie also hadn't known…and I doubted the criminal did, either. That was why they'd taken Natsunagi hostage and was trying to make us find it for them.

That said, we'd learned one thing from this situation.

"The criminal behind this is definitely a member of SPES, correct?" Saikawa asked.

"If they're asking for the ace detective's legacy, that's plenty of circumstantial evidence."

The day before, when I was talking with Charlie, she'd mentioned the possibility that SPES might be after Siesta's legacy. After this kidnapping incident, I was sure of it.

SPES was afraid of the *seed* Siesta had sown here, and they'd concealed themselves on this cruise ship to nip it in the bud. However, they hadn't been able to find the actual object. Since we were also on board and *connected* to the affair, the enemy had lost patience and tried to shake us up.

"Unfortunately, we don't have a clue what it is, either…"

So instead of searching for Siesta's legacy, we'd switched to looking for Natsunagi instead. We went around every public facility in the ship, trying to locate her. We even used Saikawa's left eye to search the cabins and other places we couldn't just walk into.

"This is the next one, isn't it?"

Our next stop was a big theater. They were going to perform a musical there that evening, and at this hour of the afternoon, a rehearsal was underway. Technically, no one was allowed inside, but we managed to use Saikawa's authority to get in anyway.

"Well? See anything?"

From her position in the very last row of the theater, Saikawa scanned the whole place. Her left eye could see through the eye patch, beneath the floor, and beyond the doors; it saw everything. If the criminal or Natsunagi happened to be in this theater, Saikawa would be able to find them instantly.

And the result was—

"Nothing. Natsunagi isn't here."

"...Okay."

If Saikawa said so, then that was that. There were still a lot of rooms we hadn't searched, though. We had to act fast, before something happened that we couldn't fix.

"Saikawa, let's go. We're running out of time."

"...Um, Kimizuka. Could you calm down a little, please?"

"We can't afford to relax. We have to find Natsunagi fast, or else—"

"Kimizuka!" As I tried to turn on my heel, Saikawa grabbed my right arm. "Kimizuka, that look in your eyes is scaring me." She was gazing at me.

For the first time, I realized there was such a thing as a gentle wry smile.

"I'm always like this," I retorted.

"That's a lie. You're normally much kinder. Lies don't work on me." Saikawa said, releasing me. "Besides, I'm sorry. Using my left eye takes... quite a bit out of me."

"...It does? Sorry about that."

That hadn't even occurred to me. If that was the case, I'd probably been pushing her a bit too hard. I closed my eyes and massaged the center of my brow, trying to reduce my anxiety.

"It's all right; calm down. Your hands squeeze. Your shoulders roll. Your breathing is rhythmic. Close your eyes, take a deep breath, then exhale. Your blood circulates. When you open your eyes, your cloudy vision will be clear."

"What was that about?"

"It's like my magic charm. I use it to calm myself down before concerts, when I'm so nervous, I worry my heart will explode. Why don't we sit down for a minute?"

I agreed to Saikawa's suggestion, and we lowered ourselves into seats in the empty house. On the stage, they were running a rehearsal for *The Phantom of the Opera*.

"I'm sorry I'm causing so much trouble. Pathetic, huh?" I muttered. I wasn't living up to my role as the older one here.

"Pathetic? Did you mean you, Kimizuka?"

"Well, I am, aren't I? When I heard Natsunagi was gone, I completely lost it...and then I started working you like a dog. I didn't even think about how it might affect you physically."

If Siesta had been alive, she would have let me have it. Assistant fail. She probably would have fired me on the spot. I'd never be able to face her.

"Heh-heh. You do say some funny things, Kimizuka."

"...I'm pretty sure I'm not brave enough to crack jokes in a situation like this."

But Saikawa was giggling, her petite body rocking with genuine amusement. "Kimizuka, you're acting so apologetic for not meeting other people's expectations, but—"

She broke off for a moment, drew a deep breath, and then:

"—I wasn't expecting all that much from you in the first place!" She pointed at me, looking triumphant.

"...Did you just roast me?"

That didn't seem right. I'd thought Saikawa and I had a pretty good, trusting relationship.

"Oh, honestly! That's not what I meant." Saikawa turned her palms up and shook her head dramatically. "That's the trouble with you, Kimizuka. You don't understand anything."

She really is making fun of me, isn't she?

"Listen, when I said 'I wasn't expecting all that much from you,' I meant it in a good way."

"Do you think you can get away with insulting people as long as you 'meant it in a good way'?"

"Regardless."

Hey, answer my question. Ugh, middle schoolers.

"I was the same way, you see."

"...The same?" I remembered my conversation with Natsunagi the day before.

"Like you, I couldn't live on my own, either."

"I couldn't live on my own." When I heard those words, something clicked in my mind.

"For me, it was my parents, and for you, it was Siesta. We both had people we couldn't afford to lose, no matter what."

And then we did.

"Once I lost the North Star of my life, I began to obsess over past promises...and then I very nearly did something I could never take back."

Past promises; irredeemable mistakes.

I couldn't ignore how this was connected to me. If I'd been in her shoes, there was no telling what I would have done. That was how important Siesta had been to me.

"But then I got a big shock. The one who saved me was you, *someone who should've been like me*...and Nagisa."

"I see. So that's why you..."

"Yes. You and Nagisa, who were as *incomplete* as I was, tried to save me. You put yourselves in my place and encouraged me to move forward. That was why I was able to take your hands so easily."

This was what had been going through her mind in her dressing room, after the attack at the concert—when she'd made the choice to put down her gun and take our hands instead. I really didn't know anything... I was an incomplete person, and a disappointment besides.

Apparently, my papier-mâché facade hadn't worked on Saikawa's left eye.

"I am really sorry, but I don't expect any more than I have to from you, Kimizuka. So please don't be any more considerate of me than you have to be. After all, that's the sort of *friendship* we have, isn't it?"

Gently, Saikawa removed the patch from her left eye. In that blue, there were no calculations, sympathy, or deceit—no impurities at all. The color was endlessly deep and clear.

"Yeah, that's fine. It's best that way."

Inwardly, I sent a compliment to Siesta, two years ago.

The idol from Japón you had your eye on is here with us right now to protect your last wish.

"But if you're the ace detective's assistant, Kimizuka, then perhaps I wouldn't mind being your assistant instead."

"The assistant of the assistant of the ace detective?"

"Yes, that's right. Like a matryoshka doll or something." Saikawa giggled as she spoke. "I don't know if I can ever be your right arm, but I believe I can be your left eye, at least."

It was a reassuring promise.

Even in a tunnel with no lights, I bet I'd be able to walk confidently, I thought.

After that, we resumed our search of the ship, until we'd been through every room.

"...We didn't find her, did we?"

The sun had set, and it wouldn't be long until the appointed hour. In the end, we had no results to show for our efforts.

"But, Kimizuka..."

"Right."

The lack of results was *the result.*

That led us to just one answer.

From here on out, no deductions or diplomacy would be necessary.

"It's all-out war, you bastard."

◆ Light in the midst of hope (despair)

When eight PM came and I went out on deck, all I saw was an expanse of black sky and black sea. Right now, except for me, there wasn't a soul around...*or so it seemed.*

Our opponent was the one who'd set the time and place, so they were bound to show. Actually, they might already be here.

I strained my eyes in the darkness.

I didn't know where they were lurking. Even with Saikawa's eye, we probably wouldn't have been able to find them. After all, our opponent had a certain *ability*.

During my conversation with Charlie, optical camouflage had briefly come up. Even Saikawa's left eye hadn't been able to locate the enemy. In that case, it had to mean they were using that sort of technique, a skill that would make them impossible to see.

And during those three years, *I'd already met this guy.*

"Enough messing around. Just get out here already—Chameleon." I glared at the invisible enemy.

You're going to give back Nagisa Natsunagi.

"Ha-ha. Now there's a fine greeting." Suddenly, a voice spoke from thin air. "I'm the one who's been waiting for you, you know. I see no one's taught you any manners since we last met."

He appeared at the very edge of the deck, with the black ocean behind him.

For a moment, the air warped and twisted, and then a human silhouette faded into view.

The lights illuminated a slim, silver-haired man with Asian features. Like Bat, he had a tentacle-like appendage, this one sprouting from his mouth.

This was Chameleon, Natsunagi's kidnapper.

His long tongue and his ability to blend in with the scenery around him and *disappear* really suited his code name.

I'd fought this guy once before, during my three-year adventure.

Back then, he hadn't shown himself at all, only hinted at his presence with his voice. This was the first time I'd actually seen him.

"As this is our first reunion in quite some time, I would love to exchange some witty repartee, but...you've kept me waiting a very long while, you see. Let's cut to the chase, shall we?"

As Chameleon spoke, a vague figure materialized in the coils of his tongue.

"Natsunagi!" I tried to run to her, but the tentacle-like tongue tightened its grip and raised her high into the air.

"Careful. Stay where you are."

"Ghk…"

The grotesque tongue, which looked as if it might be thirty meters long, carried Natsunagi over the side of the ship, holding her above the ocean.

"Ngh…"

Natsunagi seemed to be semiconscious; her eyes were closed, and she moaned as if she was in pain.

"Just hang on. I'll save you." I reached toward the holster at my waist.

"Ha-ha. Perhaps you should calm down a little."

"Shut up and get that nasty thing back in your mouth. You're not a god-damn golden retriever. At least they're cute when they do it."

Hell, you shouldn't even be intelligible with it sticking out like that.

As my irritation grew, I drew my handgun and released the safety.

"Oh-ho. You've grown quite spirited. Before, you were merely that 'ace detective's' shadow…"

"Are you trying to give me flashbacks or something? Who wanted to get down to business, again?"

…I was seething, and I needed to cool off.

"What are you after?" I asked.

Of course, I had to rescue Natsunagi fast…but I had another job to do, too.

I needed to stall for time.

Right now, the ship's passengers were escaping into the ocean in the lifeboats, under Saikawa's direction. This maneuver hinged on her charisma as the owner of the ship and as a top idol. However, it was going to take time to evacuate everyone. That was the ultimate mission I'd been assigned: Protect Natsunagi and buy enough time to evacuate all the passengers.

"I believe I've already informed you of my objective. Several times. Hand over the ace detective's legacy, if you would. Then, and only then, will I return this girl to you. No need for deadly toys," Chameleon sneered, his eyes on the gun in my right hand.

As we'd thought, Chameleon's goal—or his objective as a member of SPES—was the legacy Siesta had supposedly left on this ship. It had to be a trump card that could bring SPES down.

"I really wish I could, but unfortunately, we don't have any idea what the legacy is, either."

"Hmm. So that's your approach, is it? ...Well, I did give you free rein all day and saw nothing to the contrary. I had hoped until just a moment ago that you would find it somehow. What a pity."

So this whole time, Chameleon had been watching us from his undetectable camouflage against the scenery nearby? In that case, he had to know we wouldn't be able to trade Natsunagi's life for Siesta's legacy.

"There you have it. So can you just give her back?" I lowered my pistol, attempting to negotiate.

"I see. You do say such amusing things. Nonetheless, that would be no transaction at all. You need to offer something that will be worth my while."

"Worth your while? Well, let's see. How about this? If you release Natsunagi here and now, I won't fill your ass full of lead, and you'll be able to run back home to your mommy, safe and sound."

"...Ha-ha. You've certainly grown cheeky, haven't you?" Chameleon's bearing was as infernally polite as ever, but his eyes were clearly annoyed, and his gaze bored into me. "You seem to misunderstand your position. You do not have the advantage in these negotiations."

Chameleon's tongue squeezed Natsunagi, hard.

"Ngh...ghk...!"

"Natsunagi!"

"Kimi...zuka...?"

In the coils of Chameleon's tongue, Natsunagi opened her eyes. She looked around, and it didn't take her long to understand her situation. But she still smiled.

"...Ah-ha-ha. It looks like I blew it. I'm sorry," she murmured softly.

If her smile was going to be so sad, I didn't want to see it.

"You didn't find the ace detective's legacy. Therefore, the first condition

for exchange has been rendered invalid. We are in agreement there."
Ignoring our exchange, Chameleon made a new proposal. "In that case, I
offer you a choice between the life of this girl and the lives of the passengers and crew who are still on the ship."

"......!"

So he'd figured it out? He knew I was buying time and that we were still
evacuating the passengers from the ship. Everything. But then why...?

"What's the point of killing the passengers? What's 'worth your while'
about that?"

"Ha-ha. Firing my own words back at me? In this case, the lives of the
passengers and crew are rather incidental."

"Incidental?"

"Yes. My primary objective is merely to sink this ship. After all, the
detective's legacy is sleeping somewhere here," Chameleon said. "If we
are unable to locate it, we can still ensure no one ever will. If we cannot
obtain it, we have only to destroy it. It's extremely simple."

"...So you're saying you'll just kill the passengers while you sink the
boat?"

"Yes. It's no more than an attendant result of achieving my objective."

When I heard that, my grip tightened on the gun again. But I still had
things to ask him, so I gritted my teeth and hung on.

"Then what about Natsunagi?! What does killing her get you?!"

It was the life of a single girl. For a terrorist organization that had
even created pseudohumans like this guy, there was no point in going
after—

"That is also simple: This girl has the blood of the ace detective in her."

"......!"

My mind reeled.

Had I been right? Was it true?

SPES's main target wasn't me or Saikawa—it was Natsunagi. Not only
that, but they were only after her because she had Siesta's heart...

"Don't worry. I won't kill her so easily."

"You won't kill her...easily?" That didn't make me feel any better at all.

"Yes. After all, she holds that ace detective's heart. Human experimen-
tation, I suppose you could call it. From the tips of her toes to each

individual strand of her hair—it is worth *examining* her in detail, don't you think?"

Chameleon's eyes narrowed in a sly grin, and the tip of his grotesque tongue crawled over Natsunagi's cheek.

"—No!" Natsunagi arched backward, but the long, snakelike tongue wouldn't let her go.

I could see the agony on her face, above the dark ocean, in the grip of the tongue that stretched over the ship's side.

"Let her go, you bastard!"

This time, I really did turn the gun on Chameleon. All I had to do was pull the trigger, and I'd put a bullet right between his eyes.

"As I said, you should calm yourself a little. If you do, this girl will plunge headfirst into the ocean. It's night. You'll have no way to save her."

"Rgh…"

Yeah, I know. You don't have to tell me.

And yet my impulses wouldn't stop trying to overrule my rational brain. I held down my right hand with my shaking left hand—otherwise, it might just pull the trigger on its own.

"Now then, make your choice, if you would. Will you save this girl's life, or the lives of the many passengers on this ship? Those are your only options."

The choices he presented me with were the ugliest ones in the world.

If I rescued Natsunagi, so many other lives would be lost.

If I saved them, Natsunagi would be experimented on, then killed.

There's no way I can make that choice.

But unless I did, both worst-case scenarios were bound to become reality at once… Plus, I knew these guys. No matter which one I chose, there was no guarantee that they'd keep their end of the bargain. That was how it had been during Saikawa's incident. That was the kind of group SPES was.

Then, right from the start, my choices were—

"Kimizuka."

Suddenly, a voice called to me.

"Shoot me."

Even in the darkness, her expression was as dignified as a solitary white flower blooming proudly on the brink of a cliff.

"What are you talking about, Natsunagi?"

In the coils of the tongue, Natsunagi could only take shallow breaths, but still, she kept her gaze fixed on me, trying to make sure I knew what she thought.

"It's easy, isn't it? Think of the greater good. Or, what, have you lost your basic math skills?"

"…Since when were you so utilitarian? That's not like you."

"Really? Maybe not. Still, under these circumstances, what we need isn't my passion, but the ace detective's logic."

"You're an ace detective, too, remember?"

"No, I'm not. I'm nobody. I'm just a fake."

"That's not—!"

"Kimizuka." Natsunagi said my name again. "When you said I didn't have to be anybody's replacement—it made me happy. Thank you." She actually seemed to be smiling faintly.

If I shot Natsunagi now, the enemy would lose his hostage. After that, he'd probably try to sink this ship, passengers and all, but I'd keep him from doing that, even if it killed me. As long as he wasn't holding Natsunagi hostage, I could fire at will. Even if I couldn't hope for total victory, I might be able to manage half a victory and take him out with me.

That meant she was right.

Natsunagi's decision that I should shoot her was unassailably correct. It was the right call.

In that case. What I needed to do was—

"Kimizuka."

Natsunagi called my name, one more time.

"Shoot."

In that moment…a long-ago memory flickered through my mind.

It was the image of a white-haired girl, facing a vicious enemy all alone without telling me.

She'd never hesitated to sacrifice herself. It hadn't scared her. She was the sort of person who mistook self-sacrifice for the right choice. That's why, back then, I'd completely ripped her a new one. Even now, I had a vivid memory of her face. I'd never seen her look so stunned before.

As I remembered that scene…I thought, *Yeah, it's the same.*

Right now, Natsunagi was exactly like she had been.

And so I was sure, right now…

In that moment, when I heard what Natsunagi said, I decided on the choice I should make.

"—I don't care if it's the right call."

I could see Natsunagi's eyes widen slightly.

"Did you say you were nobody?" I took a step toward her.

Naturally, Chameleon was wary, and he made a move as if he was initiating some sort of attack—but a moment sooner, I'd aimed my gun right between his eyes.

"…Yes. All I can do is copy how some other person lived. I'm just a fake. I'm nobody."

"Is that right? Then you should be glad." I took one more step toward Natsunagi. "If you're nobody yet, that means you can become anybody you want."

If you don't know how to fly, let someone teach you how to beat your wings.

If you don't know how to live, just walk beside someone.

You spent almost eighteen years lying in bed. Running the hundred-meter dash will be way more exhilarating for you than it is for most people. This world has so much for you to enjoy and discover. From now on, you can be anybody.

"That's why I'm doing this."

I pointed the muzzle of my gun at Natsunagi.

"…My, my, we can't have that. I intend to take this girl back to our hideout and enlist her cooperation with our experiments, you know. I can't have her getting killed yet."

With a fake-looking smile on his face, Chameleon said his sickening nonsense.

But this guy had made a huge miscalculation. Not that he had any way of knowing.

On that pitch-black night, she'd made a promise to me.

"Nagisa Natsunagi can't die before I do."

Sorry, but that was the deal.

I took aim and *shot clear through the tongue* Chameleon had wrapped around Natsunagi.

"Gaaaaaaaaaaaaaaaaaaaaaaaaaaaaaaaah!"

Chameleon gave a snarling roar, and the tongue was sliced cleanly in two in a spray of blood.

Natsunagi plunged toward the dark ocean—but...

"Nagisaaaa!"

...just before she hit the black water, a small boat with a mat in it slid under her.

"Apologies for the delay!"

Yes, Saikawa. That blue eye still shone in the darkness, and it was definitely worth three billion yen.

◆ A golden banner flying in the night sky

"You say I'm no detective, but..."

I can't remember when it was, but I'd told Siesta she was more like a special agent than a detective.

"In my mind, the definition of a detective is always 'Someone who protects the interests of the client.' I take pride in that work. That's why I always have been, and always will be, a detective."

Siesta had still insisted that that was what she was.

I'm sure that when she said "client," she meant *every other human on the planet.*

She'd said that being an ace detective was in her nature, and she'd smiled. That smile was almost too bright for me.

"She's all yours now!" I yelled to Saikawa as the distant flash of memory passed.

Protect the client's interests: no more, no less. If I could just do that, it would be enough.

So what if you make a deduction? If you don't use it to save people's lives, there's no point.

Natsunagi had tried to save the people who were still on the ship at the cost of her own life. Saikawa had managed to rescue her in the nick of time. Without a doubt, they had both inherited the ace detective's last wish.

"They're gone…"

I watched the small boat race over the water; it had already carried the two girls far away.

I couldn't put either of them in any more danger. From here on, this was my job.

"You've certainly sealed your fate."

Chameleon's tone was still polite, but his formerly expressionless face was suffused with anger.

I'd seen the bullet cut off his "tongue," but he wiped the blood from his lips, then began extending that tongue again. It was like a lizard severing its own tail, then regenerating it.

And reptilian was what he was. This guy had completely discarded his humanity.

"I'll show no mercy now. I won't fail to do you the honor of killing you here."

The next moment, Chameleon's "tongue" came speeding toward me. Like Bat's tentacle, its tip morphed into a sharp blade.

"——!"

Even if I'd seen similar movement before, it wasn't an easy thing to dodge.

I tumbled, evading, but it grazed my shoulder a bit. "Ghk! Ow…"

Besides, four years ago, Siesta had been the one who'd dodged those attacks, not me. If this was how it was gonna be, maybe I really should have learned more self-defense.

"Dammit!"

In desperation, I fired at him.

To be honest, from here on out, I was flying blind.

It had been close, but I'd managed to rescue Natsunagi. And if Saikawa had come racing to us, that meant most of the other passengers must have been evacuated as well.

In that case, it was okay now. I didn't mind being the only one to go down with the ship.

"...Whew."

I was able to get to my feet somehow, then loaded more bullets into my gun. These six were the last ones.

"Well, well. Such clear resolve in your eyes. Do you intend to die alone?"

Temporarily retracting his tongue, Chameleon narrowed his eyes, shooting me a glance.

"Sorry, but no. I'm taking you with me. Two guys committing suicide together on the ocean isn't the greatest ending, but that's why nobody's hired me to write their movie."

"Even now, you can still express yourself so eloquently, hmm? I believe you may be more suited to the profession of comedian than scriptwriter. If you run a variety show in hell's second district, no doubt your audience will be showering you with tips."

Exchanging our unfunny gallows humor, we kept each other pinned down with our eyes.

"Not that I have any intention of giving you my life in the first place. In addition, those girls you *believe* you helped escape—I'll take their lives soon after I've taken yours." The way Chameleon licked his chops made my stomach turn.

"Why would you go that far...?"

Even if Natsunagi said she'd carry out Siesta's last wish, she was just a high school girl. Why would he go after her so tenaciously?

"It's all because of that heart." Chameleon's lip curled in exasperation. "I myself was only just informed of it, but—it isn't normal."

It wasn't…normal?

Was he saying Siesta's heart held some sort of secret?

"Well, there's no need for you to know. However, I will tell you that circumstances changed for us very recently."

"…What are you talking about…?"

"To my relief, apparently the situation is not as grave as we had feared. In addition, the legacy the ace detective is said to have left on this ship is about to sink with it. Victory is ours. Ha-ha, ha-ha-ha." Chameleon gave an unpleasant, mocking laugh. "After I kill you, I'll pursue those girls to the ends of the earth, the bottom of the sea, the heights of the sky. I'll torture them again and again and again, constantly, ceaselessly, until they cry and plead with me to let them die. I won't stop until the very end."

I heard something inside me snap.

"Oh dear, I fear I've spoken a bit too much. Let us finish this, shall we?"

It didn't even take me a second to realize I was going to slaughter this guy.

"Do you require time to say your prayers?"

"No. Unfortunately, I'm an atheist."

"Is that so? In that case—" Chameleon closed his mouth.

Sorry, but the end of that sentence is mine.

"—Die."

The "tongue" flew toward me like a bullet, but I slid and evaded it, getting in close to the enemy.

My self-control was gone. I jammed my gun against his jaw, but—

"How very naive." The tongue curled back in an instant like a whip, striking my hand.

"Ghk…!" I nearly dropped the gun, and while I was struggling to hang on to it—

"You're wide-open."

"Ngh… Khak…"

—that long tongue sank into my torso, and I went flying as if I'd been hit with a metal bat.

"Can't—breathe…"

I slammed into the deck, and my lungs stopped working properly. I'd probably busted a few ribs, too. I felt the blood retreating into the depths of my body, my temperature falling.

If this keeps up, I'm gonna die.

It was so abrupt. But this wasn't a hunch—it was a conviction.

"You must know a mere boy could never win against a pseudohuman."

Chameleon was coming closer. Somehow I managed to get to my feet, and I leveled my gun at him.

...But I could barely even see him.

Maybe because I was breathing shallowly, I couldn't line the sight up properly. My feet were very unsteady, too.

"There, you see? You can't protect anyone."

"Just shut the fuck up!"

I was firing at random. Most of the bullets missed their target, and the one that did fly straight at him, the guy deflected with his tongue.

So he could change its hardness at will, too, not just its length?

"You will perish here, and I will most assuredly kill the girls you helped escape with my own hands."

"...Ghk... Fuck you! Shut up!"

I set my finger on the trigger, one more time...but nothing happened. I was out of bullets.

"Yes, everything you've done has been useless. You, and those you tried to protect, will all die. Just like that damnable ace detective."

I'm going to die. That's fine. After all, I should have died a year ago. In a way, I already have.

Natsunagi, though. Saikawa.

I have to protect them, at least.

I have to protect the clients' interests, their lives.

I told Charlie I'm no detective, I'm just an assistant, but even if that's all I am—

"The ace detective's last wish...was passed to me."

To my surprise, my legs actually moved.

I remembered what Saikawa had said.

My hands squeeze. My shoulders roll.

My breathing is rhythmic. I close my eyes, take a deep breath, then exhale.

My blood circulates. When I open my eyes, my cloudy vision will be clear.

Maybe that sapphire eye had come to dwell in me. It couldn't have, not really, but what about my ears? I pinned my hopes on my acoustic system.

—And I heard it.

I wasn't the only one, either. Everyone heard that noise.

"A helicopter?"

When I looked up—there it was, in the pitch-black sky.

"Kimizuka! Get down!"

The words were so distant I wasn't sure if I'd heard them, and I threw myself onto the deck, taking cover.

In the next instant—

"Eat lead, asshooooole!!!"

Along with the ear-splitting roar of a strafe attack, a rain of bullets fell from the night sky, striking Chameleon.

"Gwaaaaaaaaaaaaaaaaaaaaaaaaaaaaaaaaaaaaah!!!"

High in the sky, in the helicopter's open hatch—

"I see you're having some trouble with that fight, Kimizuka."

—stood Charlotte Arisaka Anderson, long golden hair streaming in the night wind as she blazed away with a machine gun.

◆ Buenos días

"Charlie…"

Dazed, I looked up at the aircraft hovering in the dark sky.

The rotor blades of the armed helicopter created ring-shaped ripples on the ocean.

In the open door, Charlie was holding a machine gun, and in the pilot's seat was—

"Hey, it's been a while, you damn kid! Finally decided to turn yourself in?!" Ms. Fuubi was using the helicopter's loudspeaker to mock me.

"Anybody with eyes can see I'm the victim here!"

When I objected, Ms. Fuubi pointed at something on me.

…*Oh. Fair.*

A violation of the Firearm and Sword Possession Control Law. For the first time, she'd caught me red-handed. *Geez, she's talking like she's a proper police officer or something.*

But wasn't she the one who just brought out a military helicopter?

"It's fine if I do it! I'm a cop!"

I'm not so sure about that. Also, quit reading my mind.

Seriously. Don't make me smile. Don't reassure me; don't make me feel I'm not actually all alone yet.

"Ghk… Damn, you…"

I heard a growl that seemed to come from the depths of the earth.

Still bleeding, Chameleon got to his feet unsteadily. His narrow eyes were bloodshot, and he was gazing at Charlie and the helicopter that hovered in the night sky.

"It's been a long time, pseudohuman. I never wanted to see you again."

"Oh yeah, I recognize you…!" Chameleon's manners were slipping. This was probably what he was actually like.

"You too, Kimizuka. I thought I really wouldn't be seeing you after this, but…"

"…Tch. Were you planning this right from the beginning?"

Wipe out the enemy with force. It was a pretty Charlie-esque way of doing things.

Having sensed the enemy early on, Charlie had promptly gotten off the ship and returned with more firepower. Probably could've talked it over with me first, but... No, we'd never wasted time on that. Siesta used to give us hell for it, too.

"...Still, I'm glad you came, Charlie."

Who'd have thought the day would come when Charlie would rescue me, after all this time?

"Hmph! You can't possibly have expected me to just shut up after *a little girl like her* spoke to me like that."

"Uh, you two are the same age."

I see... So Natsunagi's words lit a fire under Charlie as well. I bet even Natsunagi herself wasn't aware of it, but there was something about her—

"Okay, Kimizuka, you stay back! It's my turn now!" Charlie called. She leveled the machine gun that was mounted near the door, taking aim at the pseudohuman again.

Too bad, huh, Chameleon? When that girl's got a weapon, dragons and tigers are no match for her.

"Go on, let's see you dance!"

With a one-liner like that, it was hard to tell who the villain was as Charlie began spraying the deck with bullets.

"...Ghk!"

Even with those injuries, Chameleon managed to dodge agilely. Every so often, he'd swing his hardened "tongue" and knock bullets away.

"Rgh! You insolent—"

It was an air-to-ground battle.

But Charlie had the stronger position.

Chameleon had his hands full trying to block the bullets raining down on him, and all he could do with his unrivaled weapon—his tongue—was defend. Faced with a never-ending storm of lead, he had no choice but to desperately run around the deck.

"Kimizuka!" Abruptly, Charlie shouted to me in a voice loud enough to be heard over the gunshots. "I hate you! I hate your guts!"

Oh, you do, huh? Well, the feeling's mutual. Sorry, but I've never even considered trying to get along with you.

"But... But! You were the one Ma'am chose! It wasn't me—it was you! So as much as I hate you...I just have to leave it to you! If the woman I loved chose the guy I hate more than anyone, then—I have no choice but to trust you, don't I?!"

Her scream was like a prayer.

She didn't let her tears show. Instead, a rain of bullets poured down from the sky.

I was sure Charlie was trying to grant her teacher's final wish.

"Kimizuka! This time, let's make this mission a success together!"

Yeah, I know. Trust me—I know.

I was planning to do that all along.

"Rraaaaaaah!"

Possibly because she didn't want to waste the time it would take to reload, instead of relying on the door gun, Charlie picked up new weapons one after another, mounting an unbroken attack on Chameleon.

If she kept pushing like this, we could win.

As I stayed under cover, I was starting to believe, but—

"—Enough."

—when she changed weapons, there was a slight pause in the attack.

Chameleon slumped, leaning forward—and abruptly vanished.

"Charlie! Watch out!"

"Huh?!"

The next instant, the helicopter tilted dramatically.

"Ghk! He got us!"

From what I could see, the rotors were fine...but something was leaking from the body.

"...Fuel, huh?"

A fluid that seemed to be gasoline was dripping from the vicinity of the engine, falling onto the deck where we stood.

The helicopter was flying significantly lower than it had been earlier. If they didn't get that altitude back, there was no telling when it might crash. However, Chameleon had completely camouflaged himself, and we couldn't see him. If things were like this, then...

"Rgh! I can't even tell whether I'm hitting him or not!"

Charlie kept attacking indiscriminately with the machine gun, but she didn't seem to be landing hits. In the cockpit, Ms. Fuubi was gripping the control stick, desperately trying to right the leaning helicopter.

Dammit, once he gained the advantage by going invisible, we couldn't even touch him.

How were you supposed to fight someone you couldn't see? If Siesta was here, what would she...?

"Ha-ha. Now your attacks won't hit me! Not even that ace detective could touch me!"

The enemy was still invisible; his triumphant voice was the only sign of him.

...Never mind that—what had he just said?

Even the ace detective hadn't been able to touch him?

Had something like that happened? How did I not know about it?

"I can see it in my mind's eye even now—that damnable girl yielding to me in humiliation!"

Oh. I see now.

It was this guy.

It was him. What happened to Siesta was because of him.

I'd finally found her mortal enemy, in the truest sense of the word.

And yet for some reason, my mind still felt calm. I had no emotions now.

All I had was the mission to annihilate SPES—to annihilate this monster.

Until that was done, I wouldn't stop moving.

"...! You killed Ma'am!" Charlie's angry shout echoed over the battlefield.

Yeah, I get it. I know how you feel better than anybody.

But, Charlie, right now, you need to look at me.

I brought two fingers up to my lips, gesturing.

"Kimizuka? —Okay. All right."

I assume you understand that I wasn't blowing a kiss.

So. Let's end this already.

It's time to slay this monster.

"I've also been thinking it's about time this woman quit smoking."

"...Yeesh. Fine, do what you gotta."

Charlie ignited the cigarette lighter she'd taken from Ms. Fuubi, then let it fall.

...Onto the deck, which was covered in the leaked fuel from the helicopter.

"Gaaaaaaaaaaaaaaaaaaaaaaaaaah!!!"

Fire blazed up all at once, burning the whole area around Chameleon. Naturally, I was in range for some damage myself. But I'd always been planning on going down with this guy if I had to.

"H-hot... G...gonna..."

Apparently, his skin's color-changing function didn't work in that harsh environment, and Chameleon's shape materialized again. He was surrounded by a pillar of fire, and he'd fallen to his knees, his long tongue hanging loosely.

"Time to die."

Then there was one dull gunshot.

With all her immeasurable emotions behind it, Charlie pulled the trigger.

"——! Gaaah!"

With an inarticulate scream, Chameleon spat up blood.

The bullet had pierced his hardened "tongue," and it fell to the deck with a clunk.

However, I could see the torn-off tongue began regenerating from the root again, and I headed toward the raging flames. Then I picked up the "tongue," which had a tip as sharp as a blade.

"——! Dammit, damn, I'll—"

The reptile in front of me was saying something.

"K...kill. You...too...shame...fully...like that...ace...detective..."

Ah. As long as that tongue kept regenerating, this thing would keep talking, huh? In that case—

"——! Ghaaaaaaaaaaaaaaaaaaah!"

I slashed through Chameleon's newly regenerated tongue, using the one I'd picked up.

This is a blade. A double-edged sword you grew yourself.

I struck again and again, shouldering the thoughts of so many people: my former partner, her comrades, the ones who'd inherited her last wish.

"Stuh...stoooooooooooooooooooop!"

Ha, as if. Maybe you should have a taste of what you did to us.

"Gaaaaaaaaaaaaaaaaaaaaaaaah!!!"

If you're going to regenerate over and over, I'll just cut through it every time. Don't ever speak again.

"Aa... Aa, aaaah..."

By now, the noises from the thing in front of me didn't seem to mean anything anymore.

But my right hand didn't stop. I hadn't done enough yet.

Bleed more, more, more.

Bleed enough for Charlie, for me, for Siesta.

Please, I'm begging you. More, more—

"—Please just die already."

I had no idea how many times I'd lopped off that tongue. Telling myself this was the last time, and praying that it would be, I raised the blade high, and—

"......!"

While the blade was still above my head, the ship lurched violently, and in the next instant—

"Not...yet."

By the time I noticed, it was too late.

"...—!"

Chameleon's long tongue was wrapped around my torso. I hadn't cut through it completely yet!

"Change...of...venue."

Then he slammed the long "tail" he'd grown into the deck.

"Ghk...!"

The burned, fragile planks fell away, and Chameleon dropped down to the deck below, dragging me with him.

"Dam...mit!"

Our midair battle lasted just a few seconds.

I was still holding the remains of that hardened "tongue," and I shoved it into Chameleon's mouth.

"Ghuh, gah!"

The tongue that had been strangling my abdomen loosened very slightly. Battered as I was, I managed to get Chameleon pinned under me somehow and let him hit the floor.

"Ow, ow, ow. Dammit, I was so close..."

Where was this? What had we fallen into?

The black smoke that billowed in through the hole in the ceiling made it hard to see, and I couldn't make out anything clearly. I'd heard Ms. Fuubi and Charlie calling me as we fell, but I couldn't hear them now.

"First off, I need to regroup…"

I had no weapon, and I didn't know where I was. I couldn't fight properly here.

Dragging my leg, I put some distance between myself and Chameleon, who was just as beat up as I was.

"…Wait, this looks a whole lot like I'm running away."

As I mocked myself in my dimming mind, I tried to figure out why I was still trying to survive after all this.

"…Natsunagi, huh?"

"I won't die. Whatever happens, I won't die and leave you behind."

Once again, I remembered what she'd said.

That's right. Since Natsunagi made that promise…I couldn't die and leave her behind, either.

After all, we hadn't even said good-bye.

When I finally reached the wall, I took another look around.

"Ha-ha, nice. Well done."

I'd been here just the day before. This place was magnificent and debauched, a seething mass of human desires, a paradise of dreams, or hell—a casino.

A truly fitting location for a final showdown.

"——, —you, —kill you."

Chameleon had regained consciousness. He got to his feet, leaning forward.

My enemy was also torn up, but my hands were empty. I didn't even have a weapon.

How was I going to fight?

…Not that I actually had any options.

"Aaaaaaaaaaaah!" Chameleon roared, and the way he looked made me wonder if he even knew who he was anymore.

Come on, bring it.

I stepped forward with my left foot, pulling my right fist back.

My weapon was my body. From this point on, it was mano a mano.

"Wooooooooooooooooooooooooorgh!" Chameleon bellowed, and his long, bloodied tongue flew straight at me.

"Rrraaaaaaaaaaaaaaaaaaaaaaaaaaaaah!" I tensed my lower body and rotated my hips.

Then, using my right arm, I wound up as far as I could, and—

"—Are you stupid, Kimi?"

I heard a voice.

At least, I thought I had.

But, I mean...there wasn't anybody around to cut into this fight, was there?

"Hand-to-hand combat with a monster? That's not just reckless. It's insane."

The next thing I heard was a gunshot—and then Chameleon's scream.

I saw a pool of blood. His long tongue had been sliced cleanly in two.

"There, now that tongue *will never be able to attack me again*."

I'd heard something like that before.

Then the owner of the voice leaped in through the hole in the ceiling and landed right in front of me.

I recognized her back. There was no way I could have mistaken it for anyone else's. Between this and that and the other, we'd barely been apart recently.

Why was she here, though? She'd gotten away on that boat a minute ago with Saikawa. Hadn't she?

It was a natural question, but a certain theory made it vanish like mist.

I was about to test that theory, but before I could, she turned around.

Then she, Nagisa Natsunagi, said:

"It's been a long time, hasn't it?"

Ah. There it is.

I'd know it anywhere. That hundred-million-watt smile was what I'd wanted to see for so long.

"Yeah. Was that enough of a nap for you—Siesta?"

◆ Those unforgettable three years I spent with you were...

The person standing in front of me was Nagisa Natsunagi. There was no doubt about that.

But.

"It's been a year since I saw your face. Your eyes look a little meaner."

What she said made it patently clear *who she was on the inside*.

"If anyone looks different here, it's you, Siesta."

She looked like Natsunagi—but inside, she was Siesta.

Ordinarily, that would have been impossible, but for some reason, I could tell this was *that sort of thing*.

If there was a reason behind it...

"So you were still in there. In that heart."

Memory transference is a phenomenon in which the donor's personality, interests, and preferences are reflected in the recipient after an organ transplant. While it hasn't been scientifically proved yet, cases of memory transference have been observed all over the world, and Nagisa Natsunagi had experienced it as well after a heart transplant.

Still, even if memory transference is a real thing, all the recipient usually picks up from the donor is their personality, their daily habits, and a few memories.

Right now, though, Natsunagi hadn't just inherited Siesta's memories. Siesta herself had taken over. As if the master and servant had switched places.

"You look like you're thinking something rude again, Kimi." Natsunagi—or rather, Siesta—frowned just a little crossly. "I'm only borrowing this girl's body for a little while. I'm not going to possess her."

Siesta was speaking in Natsunagi's voice, with Natsunagi's face.

It felt faintly strange, but even so, I said:

"It's great to see you, Siesta."

No matter how it had happened, our first meeting in a year made my knees weak—and I just dropped down onto my butt.

"Did you always smile that way, Kimi?" Siesta's eyes widened slightly.

"I may have mellowed out a bit." I did think I had, in a vague kind of way. While we were focused on our reunion...

"—Gguh, lwah."

Farther back in the casino, Chameleon was bleeding from the mouth after Siesta's shot, and he growled in a low voice. His eyes had rolled back, and the whites were bloodshot. Blue veins squirmed all through his skin. He was bending forward, tongue and tail lashing. There wasn't a trace of his human self left.

"Siesta, that's enough chitchat. We have to do something about that guy first."

"Agreed. Well, that is why I'm here anyway."

Although there was no telling where she'd gotten it, Siesta opened a silver attaché case. Inside, there was a gun for me. Then, extending her left hand to me, where I sat on the floor:

"Kimi—be my assistant."

When I heard her say it, my mind jumped back four years.

It was the same. Just like the time we'd met, at ten thousand meters.

Right now, the girl standing there was Nagisa Natsunagi—but my eyes saw Siesta as she'd been on that day, four years ago, clearly and vividly.

...In that case, this was never an actual choice.

"As you wish—ace detective." I took Siesta's hand and gave her my very best smile.

"...That expression is straight out of a horror movie."

"Leave me alone!"

We split up, fanning out to trap Chameleon between us.

"Gwooooooooourgh!!!"

Chameleon glared at us by turns, as if he was trying to warn us off. His tongue and tail writhed, attempting to catch their prey.

"Be careful! He can change the length and hardness of those however he wants!" I circled around in front of the enemy, relaying information to Siesta, who was on his other side.

"Huh? You're sure you want that side, Kimi?"

"Mm? Is there a problem with it?"

Even if this was Siesta, she was borrowing Natsunagi's body. I should be the one who faced the enemy head-on.

"His tongue can't attack me anymore, so I think having me take the front would work better."

"...I forgot."

Dammit, so much for showing off.

"I see you still haven't learned to pay attention."

"Shaddup."

Dodging the enemy's attacks, we switched places.

"Come to think of it, you always were like that." As Siesta battled the enemy's tail with her gun, she sounded nostalgic. "You'd say 'Today I'll put you up at this resort hotel' and stride into a casino and blow all the money we had."

"Ngh... Well, that was 'cause you'd cried so much the day before about how you were sick of taking dumps out in the open. I just had to; I was hoping to turn the tables with one decisive win..."

"Don't make up memories." The next instant, a bullet whizzed right past my face.

"Watch it, Siesta!"

"Would you quit trying to pin your crimes on other people? If this is about the time I accidentally saw you taking a du— Doing your business outdoors, I apologize for wounding your pride, but—"

"We're in combat right now! Don't dredge up old memories!"

I swear, this woman.

She's evading the enemy's attacks like it's easy and chatting about old times.

......

...That's what the old times were, though.

"Hey, Siesta, I've seen you embarrass yourself, too, remember?"

"What are you talking about?"

"You know—that one time? When we two lightweights drank enough liquor to fill a bathtub, and after that, we—"

"La-la-la, I can't hear you."

"I told you, don't point your gun at me!"

Whoa! Chameleon's tail smashed up a nearby gaming table, and the shards flew our way.

It was so weird.

The situation had been incredibly tense. I'd wound myself up tight over the thought that this was the final showdown...and yet, somewhere along the way, my shoulders had relaxed.

Because Siesta was here. Just fighting alongside her made my body and heart so light, it felt like I had wings.

"Kimi, did you forget we're in combat right now? Don't dredge up bad memories."

"Didn't I just say—? Yeesh, you are so unfair."

Siesta and I fired our guns in unison.

"Gaaaaaaaaaaaaaaaaaaaaaaaah!"

A direct hit. Chameleon dropped heavily to his knees.

I grabbed that opportunity to reload. "Ha-ha. That's rare. You almost never get that upset."

"My assistant is getting pretty full of himself. Since when were you the one teasing me?"

"It's like they always say: 'Give a guy three days to grow, and you might not recognize him at the end.'"

In our case, it had been a year.

We joked around with each other enough to make up for that whole year we'd been apart—or as much as we could manage anyway.

"...And? What happened after that?"

"What do you mean 'what'?"

"You know. Um..." Siesta faltered, with Natsunagi's face. "We drank liquor, we both got dead drunk, and after that, did we...y'know?"

Her expression was uncharacteristically embarrassed, and I would have loved to see it on Siesta's own face.

"Didn't you tell me not to dredge up memories?"

"Well, actually, I was so worried about it, I couldn't move on to the afterlife."

"Can we go back to the tearful reunion?"

Just then, with a growl, Chameleon got back up.

"Gohgyaaaaaaaaaaaaaaaaaah!"

It was a roar unlike any noise he'd made before, and it shook the whole room.

As if in response, Chameleon's body changed.

His vivid bloodshot eyes bulged out even further, and something like hardened scales began to sprout all over his body. With a series of dull cracking sounds, he grew far larger than any human, and his clothes ripped to shreds that barely clung to him. As if his body could no longer support its own weight, he lowered himself until he was very nearly walking on all fours, like a lizard or a dinosaur. He looked like—

"A monster." I gulped loudly.

"His 'seed' has completely taken over." Siesta came up beside me, exhaling.

"Hey, ace detective, don't bring out the jargon without explaining it first."

Geez. This was reminding me how rough those three years had been.

How many times had I ended up in hot water because she refused to tell me any of the important stuff? And then she'd ride in to save me at the very last minute, all proud of herself and demanding gratitude. Argh, just remembering it was pissing me off.

"Heh-heh. So many memories of that exact look on your face."

"You're totally mocking me, aren't you?"

"They're very fond memories, you know."

...Look, you can't just say stuff like that.

"—! Gohgyaaaaaaaaaaaaaaaaaaaaaaaaaaah!"

The monster roared again.

Yeah, I knew how he felt. He'd morphed into his ultimate form, and here we were, ignoring him. That'll make you wanna scream, all right. Just direct your complaints to the ace detective over here.

Siesta and I got back into formation, pinning the enemy between us.

"And? What did you really come back to do?"

"What? Do you want me to say I came to save you or something?"

"Man, you are not cute."

"Kidding."

Flying bullets, the smell of gun smoke—the scene was as surreal as a dream in the daytime.

Bleeding slightly from a cut on her cheek, Siesta, the daydream herself, leaped across the battlefield.

Jumping onto Chameleon's rampaging tongue, she leaped again, landing a ferocious kick on the enemy's head.

The ace detective did a single flip and touched down. "The truth is, *she* asked me to," she said as she turned around. "She said she wanted me to save you."

"Natsunagi asked you?"

"Yes. I'd planned to leave everything to her from now on, but if she was going to beg like that... You know?"

What kind of exchange had those two had, sharing the same body?

The only thing I knew was that Natsunagi's *words* had moved Siesta.

At the same time, that meant *this* was an exception. Meaning...

"So this is the last time. It won't happen again. All right?"

I could almost see the shadow of Siesta in Natsunagi's face. Her straightforward gaze was fixed on me.

"Yeah, I know."

This was our real good-bye.

"Gaaaaaaaaaaaaaaaaaaaaaaaaaaaaaaaaaaaaaah!"

The fallen, monstrous Chameleon got back up and roared.

In the next instant, he vanished. This had to be the last phase.

"Siesta, be careful," I said to her, now that she was beside me again.

"It's fine. Hang on, assistant."

"Huh? ...Whoa!"

And I was flying through the air for the first time in four years.

Siesta had saved me like this back then, too.

Pulling me with her, Siesta used her sense of smell to evade the enemy's invisible attacks.

"Apparently, letting you yank me around is just about perfect for me."

"...Where is this coming from, assistant?"

....

"Were you lonely?"

You think I'm that pathetic? No way.

"I'm sorry."
Don't apologize.

"I'm sorry for dying first."
I told you, quit apologizing.

"To tell you the truth, I hadn't actually planned to spend three whole years traveling with you."
Hey, we can't beat this guy and reminisce at the same time.
"Coming to care for somebody would have been a foolish thing to do—it would bind me to this world. I was sure it would be a fetter in the way of my work."
Like I said, focus on the fight.
There's no telling when the flames are going to make it over here.
"The next thing I knew, three years had passed. I must have taken more of a liking to you than I'd realized."
What's wrong with you?
You and I weren't lovers, and we weren't even friends.
We were detective and assistant—just business partners, in an odd way.
"I know. You didn't think of me in any special way, and I didn't treat you like anyone special. However—"
Stop. It's too late to say all that.
I can say it; that's fine. But you're not allowed.
Say I'm selfish if you want. But if you—

"Those unforgettable three years I spent with you are the best memories I have."

If you say that to me, I'll—
"Are you stupid, Kimi?" Siesta patted my head gently. "What's the point of digging in your heels with a dead girl? You did really well on your own this past year."
My throat stung, and my eyelids grew hot.

What's wrong with me? This isn't... This isn't like me at all.

Seriously, gimme a break. If Saikawa and Charlie see me like this—if Natsunagi sees me, once she's back to normal—they're gonna laugh.

I stepped away from Siesta to stand beside her.

"You're asking if I'm lonely? Sorry, but the friends I've got now are so noisy that I don't have time to think about all that." Several faces came to mind, and I gave a wry smile. "I'm not alone anymore."

"I see. Make sure you play nice with them, then."

We shifted to stand back-to-back, although it wasn't clear which of us had moved first.

It was Natsunagi's body, but I felt Siesta's warmth.

When this fight was over, she would disappear.

After she did, she'd probably never show up in Natsunagi's body again.

In that case...

"Hey, Siesta."

"What?"

"Uh, the rest of that story from earlier. We both drank liquor for the first time and got drunk, and then you asked me what happened...?"

I was pretty sure we shouldn't be having a conversation like this in what was probably the final phase of the final showdown. In a way, though, that was us in a nutshell.

We stood side by side, my outstretched right arm lined up with Siesta's left arm, so close that they touched.

"Unfortunately—or maybe not, I dunno—nothing happened."

Then we both pointed our guns straight ahead.

Our invisible enemy was bearing down on us. If we missed this shot, we were dead.

But Siesta spoke. "It's okay," she said.

Meaning there was no reason to hesitate.

Siesta had never been wrong. Not once.

And in the next instant, *a loud electronic noise rang out from the perfectly empty space right in front of us.*

"Assistant!"

"Right!"

* * *

Siesta and I both aimed at that spot, fired at the exact same time—

And then…

…a dull sound, and a brief wail, told us it was all over.

"I see. To tell you the truth, I might have slept with you once. I considered it, at least."

"Well, why didn't you say so sooner? Next time, just tell me!"

At the end, we burst out laughing like a pair of idiots.

The girls' dialogue

"You're telling me to use your body?"

The silver-haired ace detective looked bewildered.

"Yes. That's what I want in exchange for listening to your request." My voice was firm as I made my proposal.

This was a special world where only she and I could interact.

It was like a memory, or the consciousness that had been engraved on our heart, or a mere *daydream*—but it was true that I could meet her here. This was our second meeting, the first one since that fight.

"Are you sure, though?"

The ace detective looked at me steadily with those blue eyes of hers.

"This body is yours and yours alone. He said so, too, remember?"

"...Yes, you're right. These are my hands and my feet. It's all mine, from the ends of my hair to the tips of my toes. But..." I drew a deep breath. "The heart is different."

She lowered her long eyelashes.

"The heart belongs to both of us," I continued. "That means we should be able to work together, toward the same goal."

"...What do you want me to do?"

"I want you to switch with me and go save Kimizuka. He's fighting the enemy even as we speak."

"You seem to think I want to save him just as much as you do."

Urk. "—Yes, that's what I'm saying."

We had no time, but this was going nowhere. I could feel my blood pressure rising.

"Don't misunderstand. I'm already dead. I have no right to get involved with him."

In that instant, the fuse inside me was lit. "——! Arrrrrrgh, geez, you're such a pain in the butt!"

I raked my fingers through my hair so roughly that the scrunchie I'd used to tie up my side ponytail came loose and fell out.

"P-pain in the butt...? Me?"

I guess the ace detective had never dreamed anyone would say a thing like that to her; she blinked her large eyes dramatically. *Sorry, but I'm showing no mercy here.*

"You know it's true! Even in that one dream where we fought, you said *you* were the best one to be your assistant's partner, remember?!"

"That was... Listen. The upshot of that discussion was that I left my assistant to you, remember?"

"So—what? You're telling me you have no right to have anything to do with Kimizuka ever again, no matter what happens? You won't even go save him? Excuse me? What are you, a little kid?"

"...You are the first person who's ever been this rude to me." She glared at me, more irritated than I'd ever seen her.

"Huh? So now you're all fragile? Are you not used to people teasing you or something?"

"I'm leaving." The ace detective turned on her heel.

Hastily, I caught the cuff of her sleeve. "Argh, look, I'm sorry, okay? I'm sorry, so hurry up—take this body and go to him." As the mature one here, I reluctantly backed down and let her salvage her dignity.

"...Are you sure?"

"Like I said—"

I was about to tell her *I really don't care*, but...

"Will he...," she murmured. "Will my assistant think it's a nuisance? It's been so long; if I show up again now..." She seemed slightly torn. That emotion was so unlike the rational, intellectual ace detective.

"Who knows?" I replied. "Just go see for yourself."

Proof trumps argument. A perfectly apt phrase for an ace detective, I think.

"...That's just irresponsible."

She still didn't seem satisfied, and she gazed coldly at me... I hated to admit it, but that expression was cute, too. Kimizuka had acted like she hadn't been special to him, but that had to be a lie. He couldn't possibly have spent three years with an angel like this and not have developed any feelings for her. Then, what? If she was an angel, did that make me a devil? Ugh, shut up.

"Well, I mean, you suddenly started acting all blushy." I'd gotten myself upset, so I said something that would push her away.

"...I really don't think we're going to get along," said the angelic ace detective, glaring at me again.

Hrmm, I guess this turned into another fight after all. Well, this time, we shared the blame at a ratio of sixty-forty or so. Although the "forty" was mine.

"Haaah, fine, all right. All I have to do is go, correct? I just have to go." At last, turning away in a vaguely childish huff, she grudgingly accepted my proposal. "Just this once, though."

"I know. Next time... When next time comes, I'll be able to save him myself."

"...I see. All right, then." The ace detective gave a sudden smile, turned on her heel, and left.

"Say..."

As she went, I hesitated a little, but...in the end, I decided to tell her something I'd always wanted to say.

"Thank you for giving me my life—ace detective."

At that, she stopped for a moment.

"You're welcome... But I should be telling you..."

Her back was still turned toward me.

"Thank you for using *my* life—ace detective."

Epilogue

"Y-you saw Ma'am?!"

On a cruise ship sailing over the blue ocean.

On the deck, Charlie turned around, staring at me like she'd spotted a cryptid.

"Yeah. If it hadn't been for her, we'd be fish food right about now."

Later, once we'd cleared up all of the previous day's business, we'd switched to a new cruise ship the Saikawa family had procured for us and set sail for home.

The tour had been canceled. After such a major accident—major incident, really—that had been the natural decision. Fortunately, none of the crew members or passengers had been harmed. Charlie and Ms. Fuubi, who'd been in the helicopter, had managed to bail out just before it crashed, so everyone was on this ship, safe and sound.

…Almost everyone.

Chameleon had sunk into the ocean, along with his sin of taking Siesta's life.

"I see… So Ma'am saved us again."

Charlie's golden hair streamed in the sea wind, but between the strands, I caught glimpses of her profile. She was wearing a sad little smile.

"Maybe she…," she suddenly began, casually as she could. "Maybe she knew she was going to die that day."

…Yeah. Maybe she did.

I could see that ace detective in my mind, her face cool as a cucumber: *"I calculated everything, even my own death. Did you only just realize?"*

However, even if she had…

"I wanted her to live." Charlie said the words I'd swallowed down, in a voice like water spilling out of a small vessel. "But Ma'am is inside that girl...?" Her tone rose a little.

"Yeah... But she won't show herself again."

Never again. Siesta herself had said so.

"...If I pointed a gun at you right now, Kimizuka, do you suppose Ma'am would come running to save you?"

"Don't sacrifice my life to find out."

"It was a joke. I'm joking." Her expression softening abruptly, Charlie stretched. Then she turned on her heel and started to leave the deck. "Did she say anything?" she asked over her shoulder.

I couldn't see her face. What expression was she wearing?

"—She said she wanted us to get along," I said to the blond girl's back.

All I could do was relay Siesta's words.

"Oh," Charlie murmured quietly. Then, finally, she turned halfway around and spoke to me directly. "Would you come to a florist with me one of these days? I want you to help me choose what to buy."

Right. I'd heard somewhere that they didn't visit graves as often over in America.

In that case, we'd go together, someday soon. Although I had no idea whether she was actually sleeping there.

"See you later, then."

"Yeah. Later."

Yesterday's enemy is today's enemy, too.

But tomorrow, just maybe... If that's what Siesta wants.

When night fell, I headed for the cruise ship's bar.

The ship was different, so of course this wasn't the same bar, but the setup looked extremely similar. We wouldn't be discussing anything all that private today, so I took a seat at the counter and ordered a drink.

...Then, after I'd waited a little while, the person I was meeting showed up.

"Sorry to keep you waiting," said Nagisa Natsunagi, sitting down next to me.

While she ordered her drink, I watched her out of the corner of my eye. She wasn't dressed to the nines the way she had been last time. Instead, she was wearing her usual baggy T-shirt and shorts.

Well, thinking about it, I shouldn't have been surprised. That low-cut dress was probably at the bottom of the ocean by now.

Before long, our drinks arrived, and we clinked our glasses together lightly.

"And, um, what exactly are you wearing?"

...Dammit, she wasn't gonna let it slide, huh? And here I'd avoided describing it.

"We never seem to be quite in tune, do we?"

I just assumed you'd be all dressed up again.

"What's with that jacket? It looks strange on you."

"I had Saikawa buy it for me."

"Wow, what a turnoff. Seriously, yikes."

Hey, quit making valid points. You know I have no comeback for that.

...Well, she was the same Natsunagi as always. By now, I couldn't see a trace of Siesta in her.

After that, once we'd defeated Chameleon...

...Siesta (Natsunagi) and I had thrown ourselves from the sinking ship into the ocean, barely escaping with our lives. We'd apparently clung to broken planks and drifted until a rescue boat picked us up.

I say "apparently" because we'd both been unconscious when we were rescued, and by the time I woke up, we were already on this cruise ship.

And when I'd opened my eyes, Natsunagi was already...Natsunagi.

When I asked her, she said she didn't have any memories from the time when Siesta's personality had taken over. Siesta herself was taking another one of her famous naps.

"Say, Natsunagi."

"What?"

There was no sense in dragging it out forever. Steeling myself, I brought up the reason I'd called her here.

"Can I ask you to keep on being an ace detective?"

Would she still carry out Siesta's last wish for her, even after getting dragged into an incident like this one?

Did she plan to become an ace detective in the truest sense of the word, instead of just pretending?

We would be fighting SPES more frequently from here on out.

If she turned me down, I couldn't blame her for it. But I did have to know for sure.

"...To be honest, I'm really not sure about this." Natsunagi traced the rim of her glass with a slim finger. "I was useless back there. As a matter of fact, I only made trouble for everybody, and you and Yui had to rescue me. In the end—I leaned on this heart. On *her*." Her voice dropped to a murmur. "I knew it. I'm really not..." She forced a smile.

"You know that's not true."

"...Kimizuka?"

"That *ringtone* completely saved our butts."

During the fight with Chameleon, that electronic noise had ultimately told us where he was. The sound had come from Natsunagi's phone; she'd slipped it into Chameleon's clothes when he'd snatched her. It had been an impulsive idea, a way to fight an enemy when our eyes were useless.

"...I see. That only worked because Yui and Charlie helped, though."

From what I heard later, while Siesta and I were fighting Chameleon, Charlie had piloted a small boat carrying Yui, who had used her left eye to watch the battle unfold from out on the ocean. Then, when Chameleon disappeared, she'd called Natsunagi's phone so that the ringtone could tell us where he was. Siesta had also anticipated everything— which meant that, once again, I was the only one in the dark.

...Still, I guess that's okay. I am the assistant, after all.

The important thing was Natsunagi.

Could she fill the shoes of the ace detective?

"Besides, Natsunagi, *Siesta herself told me* you'd loaned her your body of your own volition. What you said was why Siesta acted, and that saved my life."

Without that passion of hers, I would have died. It was Natsunagi who'd saved me.

On top of that, she had a natural gift that even she hadn't noticed.

During that first incident with the heart, I'd had feelings I hadn't acknowledged—that maybe I'd even repressed—and Natsunagi had lit a fire under me, reminding me of the mission I needed to carry out.

During the sapphire incident, Natsunagi saw what Saikawa actually wanted before I did, resolving the issue without resorting to force.

Then, during this incident, she'd used her emotions and words to get Charlie and me, and even Siesta, to act. I was sure Natsunagi had the ability *to say and do* the things people wanted most at any given moment.

In that case—

"Thank you. You make the best ace detective ever."

After all, it's true, isn't it? Because detectives exist to fulfill their clients' requests.

"...That's not fair," Natsunagi murmured softly.

I didn't know what exactly she was referring to, but from the way her lips curved slightly, we seemed to have avoided a breakdown of negotiations.

"But... Yes. I'll do it. Besides...," Natsunagi went on. "Someone asked me for a favor, too."

"Someone? Don't tell me—Siesta?"

"Yes. That was her condition for going back to work. Just this once."

Then Natsunagi told me about the contract she'd secretly made with Siesta.

"Nagisa Natsunagi, Yui Saikawa, Charlotte Arisaka Anderson, and Kimihiko Kimizuka—I want the four of you to defeat SPES."

"The four of you are the legacy *I left—and the last hope."*

"That's what she told me," Natsunagi said, smiling softly.

"I see," I said briefly and nodded.

I was sure that, right now, in this instant...

...I'd finally taken up the ace detective's last wish as well, in the truest sense of the word.

"Well, that doesn't change the fact that I'm not sure of myself." Smiling wryly, Natsunagi raised her glass to her lips.

"It's fine. Nobody's got less confidence than I do."

"What an awful comparison. Would anyone ever feel better after hearing that?"

"Besides, you sound like you think Siesta's this perfect superhuman, unlike you, but she's actually not."

"Really?"

Yes, really. Sorry, Siesta. Dead men tell no tales.

"She wasn't a drinker, but this one time, she drank, like, a whole bathtub of liquor, got dead drunk, and then—"

That was when, out of nowhere, Natsunagi picked up her drink and chugged it, all at once.

"Hmm? Hey, Natsunagi?"

The lights in the bar were dim, but when I took a close look at her face, her cheeks seemed to be red.

And then—

"This actually had alcohol in it, didn't it?" she said.

Suddenly, Natsunagi set a finger on my chin, tilting it up. I couldn't fight back... It was as if she was reenacting the day we'd met, in the classroom after school.

"Ngh, ghk..."

"So. You're coming to my room today, aren't you?"

"...Huh? What are you talking about?"

—No, wait. Could *the real Natsunagi* say that sort of thing?

In that case, this was... No, but it couldn't be...

"Which do you think it is?"

...Haaah. That smile's completely against the rules.

As I was struggling to come up with an answer...

"Erm, attention all passengers."

It was a shipboard announcement.

Unlike the earlier criminal statement, this one was apparently official, made by the captain.

"*While I can't disclose the details...,*" the announcement began, very enigmatically.

"*...is there a detective on this ship?*"

I exchanged glances with *her*, the girl next to me, and we both nodded. It was still too soon for an epilogue.

Afterword

It's a pleasure to meet you. My name is nigozyu, and they've been kind enough to give me the Best Prize in the 15th MF Bunko J Light Novel Rookie Award.

...Right off the bat, I'd like to start with an apology: I was terrible at adjusting the number of pages, and so, incredibly, this afterword is three whole pages long. Since it is an afterword by a humble rookie light novelist, feel free to skip the whole thing with élan, then use those extra few minutes to tweet or post your thoughts on the book you just read on social media. (Ingenious advertising.)

All right, now that we've gotten the foreword of the afterword out of the way: Once again, thank you very much to all the readers who picked up *The Detective Is Already Dead*.

If the title made you hope that it was going to be a genuine mystery, I probably owe you an apology, but nothing could make me happier than if you managed to enjoy it as an entertaining blend of genres.

The spark for this novel was a single sentence that popped into my head: "Is there a detective on this plane?"

At the time, even I had no idea the book would turn out to be such a hodgepodge of genres. However, when I was giving some fresh thought to my concept of light novels, the first thing that came to mind was "anything goes."

In that case, couldn't I incorporate all the genres I thought were fun, and wouldn't it be okay if I built the story around the parts I wanted to write most: the conversations and relationships between the protagonist and the heroines? When I sat down at my computer with that thought in mind, the result was this novel.

Was the experiment a success or a failure? I'll have to wait for the reader reviews to come in before I know for sure. Given that they let me release it as a book, though, I don't think the time I spent typing away based on that resolution was a waste.

Ordinarily, this would be the perfect place to start wrapping things up, but I have a page left to fill, so please stick with me a little longer.

This is rather abrupt, but do any of you ever think that life might just be too hard? I do. I think it first occurred to me around the time I dropped out of kindergarten (I'd encourage you not to drop out of kindergarten), so by this point, I've lived with that thought for more than twenty years.

I was the sort of kid who couldn't do the things my friends managed to do as a matter of course, and so I ran into all sorts of hardship in all sorts of places. I'd spend my days sitting in corners, hugging my knees and shifting the blame off over the horizon: "It's not my fault, it's society's fault, it's the country's fault..." Whenever I felt that way, light novels got me through it... Y'know I thought if I followed that train of thought, I might be able to wrap this up on a feel-good note, but actually, it doesn't have much to do with anything.

I first encountered light novels after I'd flunked my college entrance exams and started attending a cram school, but I couldn't work up any enthusiasm for it and was skipping school at a bookstore. (Am I garbage?)

After that, I continued smoothly failing to engage with the rails of a proper life, and sociability has been a foreign concept to me for a very long time. However, writing a novel and releasing it into the world has been a valuable experience. While putting it this way may get me scolded by society at large, I've been spending my days thinking, *My life really is like the Game of Life.*

Now then, since I opened with an apology, I'd like to close with thank-yous.

First, my supervising editor, O.

I had a very hard time clearing the hurdles my editor set for me, and I'm currently making a nuisance of myself in the present progressive tense, for which I'm terribly ashamed. There are lots of characters and developments in this volume that wouldn't even have been there without O, and I'm seriously grateful. Really, thank you so much. Please continue to help me out.

Next, the illustrator, Umibouzu.

The artist dexterously picked up elements from my clumsy concepts and prose and created truly wonderful characters, and even now, as I'm writing this afterword, I have no idea how to express my gratitude. I should probably pull together about seven hundred million yen from my pocket money, shouldn't I? Or that's what I thought, but the illustrator blurb only says, "I want to eat bean sprouts," so maybe that would be better. Thank you so much for being in charge of the illustrations.

In addition, once again, let me thank everyone who was involved in the publication of this book, the four authors who acted as judges for the Rookie Award, my family, my friends, and the readers who supported me—thank you very much.

Finally, I have an announcement to make, so please see the next page.

"Why don't we do something
frivolous once in a while?"

"When did
you two
get to be
in that
sort of
relationship?"

"Heh-heh.
This is the first
time we've slept
together like this,
isn't it?"

"I won't go
off and die
without
telling you.
—I swear
I won't."

"It's safe to assume
you'll never see me
in an apron again."

"For example, about one month from now, you'll
regain that routine you've been longing for and
begin living as a normal high school student."

On that day, the detective died.

The Detective Is Already Dead 2
Coming fall 2021

"All right, the detective is

"Jack the Ripper has risen again. I want you to help us capture him."

"I'm constantly overworking my brain,

It was the truth of the ace detective's death.

so my three great drives are a bit

A record of the long yet brief journey of the

stronger than those of other people."

detective and her assistant.

"It's just as you say: We have comrades all over the world. In politics, finance, the police, the clergy... It's quite possible that someone right next to you is actually a member of SPES."

"You are an angel;

I'm a monster.

That's fine.

It's what I've

always wanted."

"I entrusted my most important possession to a man I hadn't seen in a very long time."

already dead. What will you do?"